PLEASE HER

The Life and Times of David Orion

MACKENZIE MASTERS

For C. who knows a Unicorn when she sees one.

PROLOGUE

DAVID

"How do you feel?"

Laura exhaled a long breath and nodded, satisfaction twisting the corners of her mouth upward.

"I can honestly say that I've never, ever had an experience like that before."

We dressed. Since my preparation was simpler than hers, I sat on the bathroom counter and watched her apply makeup, adjusting the minutiae of her executive uniform.

"You know how to display the brand," I said with the hint of a chuckle.

She didn't take her eyes off of the mirror as she applied the last of her mascara. "It's not as easy as it used to be."

She was back in character.

I circled the edge of her ear with a finger. "I'm glad I got to get a small taste of the wonderful woman behind the mask."

She turned to examine me. The authenticity returned. "Thank you. I had forgotten that part of who I am. I'll never stop chasing my dreams. But you reminded me that intimacy doesn't need to be a casualty of that quest." Her voice was earnest; all traces of disbelief about my unique profession were gone.

Laura scanned what she saw in the long mirror on the back of the door to the hotel's executive suite, curling the name tag lanyard around her neck. I gently closed one more button on her blouse, exposing a little less cleavage.

I kissed her forehead. "Win him first with your mind, then with your heart."

She pulled at the lapels of my sport coat, depositing my fee, in cash, into the breast pocket.

Laura took one last taste of my mouth. "You provide an excellent return on investment, David. I may require your services again."

"I'm retiring," I said. "This is the last dance."

A different woman answered me. Cold, indifferent. It was as if all that Laura and I had just shared no longer existed. She shrugged.

"That's a shame."

I gave her cheek a last caress. Her cell phone vibrated. She must have recognized the number.

"I'll need an earlier flight tomorrow, Nadine. Preferably the 7:55 through O'Hare." Laura popped in an earpiece and flipped her smart phone screen to reveal a calendar.

I was invisible.

Leaving her room to return to the bar. I checked my Rolex as the elevator door opened, ready to close an eventful chapter that had begun a decade earlier. Five minutes to spare before my next appointment.

She never showed. I took it as a good omen.

༖ I ༖

ELLEN

F IVE YEARS EARLIER...

DAVID

Late March in the Midwest gives you hope. The days are warmer, it's not pitch dark when you wake up, hints of expectant green emerge from beneath snowdrifts. For a college senior, it's a manic depressive moment. You are closing the page on a youth you now wish had lasted a little longer. The anticipation connected to starting a career is seductive. But always lurking in the background are your student loans. For this reason, you rationalize, you don't miss an opportunity to party when someone else is paying.

I met Ellen Corbin the day after my twenty-first birthday.

I was never prone to hangovers. In fact, on that morning, I was still feeling the glow from the late evening of celebration where my friends had plied me with cocktail after cocktail.

While my blood alcohol numbers were definitely in the safe zone, my normal professional defenses were thin as I pulled my pickup into the driveway of a modest home in a tree-lined neighborhood near campus.

The woman who answered the door was still in her bathrobe. She was blonde, five foot nine, one hundred and thirty perfectly proportioned pounds. Her blue eyes looked like they had been crying. Her wet hair told me she was fresh out of the shower.

I held up an ID card, confirming that I was the "cable guy" and offered to come back when she was in a better position to receive visitors. She motioned me in with a tired smile and pointed to the problem television in her living room.

The relationship between people and technology is often complex. Troubleshooting electronics frequently required troubleshooting an operator error. I inspected the place for signs that might reveal my customer's backstory. Several packages of diapers and a small bassinet were among an assortment of partially unpacked boxes.

I began examining the connections. "Are you moving in our moving out?"

Her eyes focused on infinity. Tiny wrinkles at their edges made her look older than her years. But her voice was clear and calm. "Moving in."

She paused for a minute, perhaps unsure of how much she wanted to share. She sat on the couch, her robe barely covering an exquisite body for a woman so recently pregnant.

"My husband just filed for divorce." She choked on the word. "We were struggling and thought a baby would strengthen our relationship. It turned out to end it."

I stopped concentrating on the job at hand and sat on the floor, facing her.

"I'm so sorry."

She tried to wave it off. "Please don't be. We were never a good fit. And," she pointed to one of the two bedrooms, "I got a beautiful daughter in the process."

A child without a father touched a nerve. I tried to sound empathetic. "I'm afraid I know more than my share of divorced people. Sometimes these things turn out to have happy endings."

Her eyes were wet. "I hope so. The transition has been hard. Elise—that's my daughter's name—Elise and I are pretty much on our own. My parents think the failure of our marriage is my fault."

She pressed her exquisite breasts, tastefully hidden beneath her robe together, punctuating the move with a slight groan of discomfort.

"And the hormones are driving me crazy. My moods sway back and forth like a swing set at the park."

A hand covered her mouth as if some unseen force had decided that she was revealing a little too much about her personal problems.

"But you need not hear about my troubles. David, is it? Tell me about you."

Embarrassment colored my cheeks as I realized that the curve of her hips and the way she was sitting were distracting me. I went way beyond the brief paragraph in my LinkedIn profile.

"My name is David Orion. I'm a senior at the university, majoring in business. I'm an orphan. My parents died when I was in junior high. I grew up in a series of foster homes over the next four years. Not all were good. But I was always grateful for a roof over my head. I work days at the cable company and am finishing my degree at night. And I don't know what I want to be when I grow up."

"Who does?" she said. The hint of a smile tickled her cheeks. "Being a grownup is overrated."

Why did I feel compelled to share so much with a stranger? Was it the remnants of the booze? Or was it something else?

She pointed to the service award patch on my shirt. "You must be good at what you do."

I felt myself blush. "I try to work fast and get things done right the first time, ma'am. Let me take another look at this work order to see what it tells me."

It wasn't a repair call. They had disconnected her for non-payment at a previous address, and the company had mistakenly let her activate here. My job was to tell her she couldn't have cable unless she paid up.

I knew what it was like to be broke. Here she was with a new baby and nothing to keep her company.

An idea came to me. "Let me run out back and check the wiring."

When I got out to the truck, I called my buddy in the billing department.

"Hey, Jerry. If I give you my credit card, can you wipe a customer's back charges for me? She's a new mom, and her husband just walked out on her."

My friend knew that my generosity often overdrew my bank balance. "Like you even have enough credit left to cover this. She owes over four hundred dollars!"

That would definitely max out my card. But I couldn't get her face out of my mind.

"Run it. If there's not enough, can you spot me some until payday?"

"You're always doing this, David. It has to stop, or you'll be the one who is getting disconnected."

"Do me a favor," I said. "Remember a time when you thought the world was crashing down and nobody seemed to care. I bet someone showed up and helped you through it. Let that memory roll around in your head and then run my damn card."

I could hear keystrokes clicking on the other end of the line.

"Dang, what a shit heel. Her soon-to-be-ex old man stopped payment on a check, just to turn the knife. Geeze, it's Bradford Stanton."

I knew the name. "Stanton, Weber, Preston, and Stevens."

Jerry whistled. "The four horsemen of the apocalypse. I pity that woman. Those guys will leave her barefoot and broke."

"Hmm," I said. "Maybe it's time to call in my marker."

"Kyle McClellan?" Jerry was incredulous. "You don't even know this woman, and you want to burn your favor with McClellan?"

"Yeah." I tried to sound casual. "Get me his number."

"Dave..." Jerry tried not to sound patronizing. "You saved his daughter's virtue. He promised you a Vito Corleone favor. You don't spend that lottery ticket on a stranger. And another thing. McClellan probably plays golf with Brad Stanton. They might be best friends."

I hated bullies. That woman's husband was one of the worst. The scene from two years prior started to play back in my mind.

Jerry and I ended up at a frat party. It definitely wasn't my thing, but I indulged my buddy, and we found ourselves knee-deep in entitled rich boys and drunk sorority girls. Jerry had a cousin who was a brother, or whatever those guys call one another. The dude invited us up to the chapter president's room, and there she was, Piper McClellan, spread eagle on a king-sized bed, stoned senseless on Rohypnol.

There was a line of frat boys waiting to take their turn between her legs after the prez had his way with Piper. Jerry's cousin had wanted to know if we wanted in on the action.

I had witnessed what roofies could do in a couple of foster homes before I was old enough and strong enough to do something about it. I didn't know Piper from Adam but seeing her helpless and unable to assert her will made me assert mine.

When the chapter president dropped his pants, I lost my temper and shoved his skinny ass away from the bed.

That got the attention of the chapter sergeant at arms, a linebacker type. "Hey, asshole," he said in his toughest voice. "You're a guest here. Don't get involved in something that's none of your business."

"Tonight, she's my business," I said, surprised at the menace in my voice. "I just decided we're going steady. She's my girl now, so you all can take your needle dicks somewhere else."

I couldn't say that my fists were black belt worthy, but it's hard to stop someone who is blind angry, and since most of the conga line already had their pants to their knees, Jerry and I had enough of an advantage to put the majority of them out of action before one of the other female guests heard the commotion and dialed 9-1-1.

We were able to drag Piper out of the place before the cops got there. When her father heard the story, he summoned me to his private study. He wanted names. I didn't give any up, but I made a friend for life and got a godfather promise to return the favor if I ever needed one.

Mr. McClellan chuckled when I mentioned Bradford Stanton's name. "Yeah, I know Brad personally. He's one of my closest..." McClellan paused. "Closest friends. But you know what friends are in my business—enemies waiting to cut your nuts off if it benefits their interest. Send the wife my way. We'll make Bradford Stanton regret he ever married her."

I wondered if spending a golden ticket for a stranger was good judgment. But something I couldn't yet understand made it feel really good.

"Okay," Jerry said after I came back on the line. "I created a new customer account that separates her from that rat bastard. I'll send the collections guys after his ass. And let's give her, say, two months' credit for the inconvenience."

It pays to have friends in low places.

"Thanks a million, partner. Meet me after work, and I'll spend some of my remaining credit on you."

"I still think you're an idiot for tossing that brass ring away for someone you just met."

I climbed the utility pole in the backyard and reconnected the wires.

When I returned to the living room, the TV displayed a perfect picture.

"The trouble was outside, ma'am. Before I go, let's make sure your favorite channels are working."

She fumbled with the remote control. "I've never been able to navigate these stupid things. Do you mind sitting next to me in case I mess something up?"

She patted the cushion with a manicured hand.

I hesitated. Broken women were unpredictable.

"It's okay. I promise not to bite."

Her tone communicated a clear subtext. It made me excited and uneasy at the same time.

I unstrapped the tool belt from around my waist and took a seat, maintaining enough physical space to avoid making us both feel awkward.

She moved closer. Perhaps she was grateful for the proximity of a friendly face. In the process, her robe loosened. It revealed an exquisitely stiff nipple and just enough of her nether regions to confirm she was a natural blonde.

She manipulated the remote control and began scanning the

lineup.

"How busy is your schedule this morning?"

My head was spinning. On the one hand, the college-boy hormones were in overdrive. On the other, I felt something new, a fascination with the aura that surrounded this woman. It was strength and weakness, fear and confidence, a tempting emotional force field that encircled me and pulled me toward her.

I fought the sensation, producing the pager that dispatched my service calls.

"I wait for this thing to go off and head where it tells me to."

"And when it doesn't go off?"

"My schoolbooks are in the truck. I find a quiet parking spot and try to stay ahead of my homework."

She ran her hand along my arm, feeling the muscles beneath my uniform shirt. I was self-conscious about the prominence that was visible behind my zipper. Was she smiling because of my dedication to academia or because she could see the unmistakable topology down below?

"You're quite the boy scout, David."

"Far from it. I have more than my share of flaws."

"Flaws are the new sexy," she said. Her mood darkened. "At least I'm trying to convince myself that's the case. Rationalizing bad decisions has become an art form."

I tried to think of something supportive to say. Her aura vibrated between a hopeless black and the rainbow I associated with healers. "Time heals wounds and wounds heels. It may not feel like it in the moment, but in my experience, it always works out that way."

She was looking at me differently now. I would come to recognize that look in a hundred faces. But in this moment, it was new, unfamiliar, disturbing.

"You must have other hobbies besides school. A girlfriend?"

"You're fishing."

She nibbled at the bottom of her lip. "Shut up! I'm being a good hostess. Indulge me."

The twinkle in her eye was appealing. She had a sense of humor.

"No girlfriend at the moment. Although several auditioned for the role last night. Birthday hijinks. A few too many cocktails. I look especially attractive on the third gin and tonic."

She switched off the TV and turned to face me.

"I'll be honest with you. My husband stopped having sex with me after I conceived. Elise is three months old so that makes it nearly a year since I've felt the excitement of having a man inside of me."

Her provocative confession threw me way outside of my comfort zone.

I backed away.

"Listen, ma'am, I appreciate the sentiment. And you are the most attractive woman I've seen, drunk or sober, in a long time. But I really need this job. I can get into a lot of trouble for what I think you are implying."

She leaned forward, brushing a nipple against my shirt. "My name is Ellen. It will be Ellen Corbin when I divorce that scumbag and get my identity back. And if you don't fuck me right now, I'll call your office and tell them you did."

Ellen seized my face and kissed me. Hers were fervent almost to the point of desperation, intermingled with sighs of satisfaction. I attempted to resist. But her eagerness was just too compelling. I kissed back.

"You slobber when you kiss."

For a moment, her sadness vanished. "Wait till you see me in bed."

Her hands began to explore the contours of my body.

I could feel her desire building. "Is this how you treat all your tradespeople?"

She ran a finger along the thick bulge that pressed against my jeans. "Five Stars on Angie's List."

I had made out with many young women. Ellen's experienced approach took me to a whole new level. It cornered me. My willpower was weak from my evening of drinking. It, combined with the urgency of her desire, overpowered my inhibitions.

She took another look at the result, pleased by my still-growing interest.

Ellen Corbin took my hand.

"I want to see what you look like naked."

I tried one last feeble attempt to escape. "What about your daughter?"

"She went to sleep just before you arrived. We both want this. Stop fighting it."

⌘

THE KING-SIZED BED SEEMED TO FILL ALMOST EVERY INCH OF THE small master bedroom.

Ellen removed my uniform shirt and unzipped my pants, motioning for me to take them off. "If there is any hassle at your work, I'll back you up. 'The customer is always right!' Now, lie on the bed and let me feel you inside of me."

Ellen caught her breath when my manhood was revealed. "Holy shit. You must be very popular with the girls."

I tried to sound more mature than I felt. "It's not something I share with just anybody."

She pushed me backward onto the mattress. "This is gonna be great."

I was ready to go there and then. But from out of the past, I could hear my last foster father whisper a warning. "When you enter a woman without your armor, every other person who has made love to her becomes part of you. Trust me, David. For both of your safety, never do the deed without protection."

"I have one rule, ma'am. I mean, Ellen. I never go out in the rain without my rubbers."

I retrieved a condom from my wallet and held it out in the palm of my hand, turning my hips so that my full engorgement was pointing toward her.

"Would you like to do the honors?"

"Definitely," she said. "But first, let me taste that popsicle."

Her robe fluttered to the floor. An instant later, her mouth was surrounding me.

"This," she said between some of the most erotic slurping sounds

I ever heard, "is a little fetish of mine. For some reason, my soon-to-be ex-husband didn't like oral sex, either."

She stopped for a moment. "He said it was 'ugly' and 'dirty.' Talk about killing your self-confidence."

"Your husband is an idiot," I said. "Where were you when I was thirteen?"

"Twenty-three and blowing all the wrong guys. Were you this big then?"

"It's a family trait. My mother had a female OB. She fainted in the delivery room."

Ellen resumed her work, never taking her eyes off mine, alternating powerful swirls of her tongue around my head with deep plunges down her throat.

At first, she measured her pace, but as Ellen gained confidence, it quickened. When she wrapped a fist around me, I lost all control and came.

Hearing her eagerly gorge herself on the warm product of my orgasm only made me want her more.

When I finished, she was gasping for air. "That was a huge load, young man."

"At my company, we are trained to under-promise and over-deliver."

I admired her delicate face and the flowing blond hair that cascaded over her shoulders. But it was her deep-blue eyes that held me under their spell. Beyond my smart-ass bravado, I was beginning to feel something for this woman that went beyond the physical. Her attitude was disarming, her skills were olympian, and I always fell for the helpless.

"How can I please you?" I asked.

"By letting me please you."

Ellen rolled on top of me. She hovered above, now eager and effervescent.

She applied the condom and closed her eyes, perhaps evoking a long-past romantic memory. Slowly, she lowered her beautiful body to become one with mine. The warmth of her, coupled with what I imagined was going on inside her head, was too much. I came again, arching upward with each heaving ejaculation.

Ellen giggled like a schoolgirl. "I guess I still have some skills. And you, David, have quite the stamina."

I challenged her. "If I'm going to lose my job, I want to make it a memorable disaster. Are you going to get serious about this, or are we just playing around?"

Ellen bent over and rubbed her nose against mine. "I'm just beginning."

She kissed me again, her agile tongue dancing with my own as her beautiful breasts pressed against my chest.

Ellen did not neglect her efforts below. She glided her hips up and down. I was increasing in both size and girth inside of her. The point of her own exhibition rubbed against my pubic bone.

She pulled her head back slightly, closing her eyes to focus again on her rhythm. She, too, was in excellent physical shape. She showed no signs of fatigue, just a fierce concentration on her work.

My fascination with her focus was something new. It was as if I had left my body and was watching the whole thing from above. In that moment, I discovered for the first time that I could control my own cravings. This could become a superpower central to my ability to please a woman. A wave of elation flowed through me. My self-confidence soared. A switch flipped in my head, and I now focused my sole concentration on helping her come.

I grasped her hips, rising to meet her thrusts. She began to cry. The sound intensified with each cycle. Her breathing synchronized with her movements. Her whimpers transformed into what felt like angry outbursts. I wondered if she might be channeling months, perhaps even years, of anger and despondency into this moment.

The combination of psychological and sexual stimulation reached a peak. Ellen experienced what I could only describe as a volcanic orgasm. She arched her back, digging her fingernails into my ribs as she slammed her hips against mine. Ellen contracted, pulling me deeper into her.

But what made me catch my breath was the wail. It was a plaintive cry that seemed to come from the deepest corners of her soul.

The pulsations continued within her. Ellen fought to rein in her emotions. It was a losing battle.

She fell into my arms and sobbed. Waves of pain and sorrow flowed from her. She pounded the mattress on either side of me with her fists.

I held her tightly but tenderly, her head resting on my chest until her fury at last dissipated.

When she regained her composure, she rolled off of me and lay on her back.

She took a deep breath, accenting each of her words as if it were a sentence.

"That. Was. Amazing."

Ellen turned to face me, propping her head onto a pillow. "I never realized how much pain, regret, sorrow, and anger I've been holding onto." She twirled a lock of my hair. "And to have a young man ravish me? What great therapy! Oh, God! It's the best sex I've had in my entire life."

That was the case for me. I cared about Ellen. I still didn't understand how such deep feelings could arise so quickly. But I felt immense satisfaction in being able to alleviate her suffering. It was a new sensation, something I wanted to feel again.

All my twenty-one-year-old mind could muster was, "I'm so sorry, Ellen. I don't know what to say."

Her mood seemed suddenly euphoric. She pulled me toward her.

"Say nothing. Fuck me again until we both come together. I'll show you how."

She was now a different woman: confident, experienced, and eager.

She took my hand in hers.

"Pay attention."

I did.

"Put your thumb and index finger on either side of my love button."

She giggled when she said, "love button," as if it had just become part of our own private lexicon.

"Press them together, gently, to raise it. Good! Now lick me from side to side."

I had to admit that this was effective. Ellen put her hands on the top of my head, guiding my movements. Her little moans told me when I was on the right track.

"That's it. A little more speed. Lighter. Now purse your lips and add a bit of sucking between the tongue dancing."

She trembled as her teachings had their intended effect.

"Okay, Okay." She lifted my head so we could again make eye contact. "Remember this. It's a little skill that will serve you well."

Ellen spread her legs, cupping her breasts in her hands for my visual benefit.

"Now, let's learn the right way to do missionary."

She allowed her tits to slide outward toward the edges of her chest. The movement was a huge turn on.

"Ready?"

I was more than ready.

Ellen pressed her hands against my thighs and guided me into her.

"The trick is to start slowly, like this." She moved my full length in and out of her, occasionally rubbing the tip on her clit. "When you get good at this, you won't need my hand. We like it when men start gradually, gently entering us and pulling all the way out to tingle our triggers."

She paused, and our gazes locked. It felt as if she could see into the very depths of my soul, as if she knew everything about me, perhaps even better than I knew myself. She seemed to make a decision. And then, I could see a new feeling on her face. Gratitude.

Her expert hands guided me with increasing speed and strength.

"What about the condom?" I said. "It's already full. Won't it break?"

She shook her head, wordlessly focusing me on her teachings.

There was no pulling out to rub her clit now. She kept increasing the pace and depth of my thrusts.

"Look at me," she commanded. "Pound me as hard as you can with that gorgeous body. Fuck me. Fuck me like it's your first time."

Her face was a portrait of self-assurance and resolve. Her rapid breathing was a sign that she was close to climax. I was ready to go on a nanosecond's notice.

"Almost there?" she asked.

I nodded. "I got this, Ellen. Go for it. Come for me. Come for me whenever you're ready. I'm here for you. I'm proud of you."

The combination of the words and the friction took her there. She threw her arms around me, pulling me to her as we both climaxed at the same instant. I watched her eyes roll back into her head, resolving to perfect the new skills she'd taught me.

"That's it," she panted. "That's it. You're an excellent pupil, David. You've just passed lesson one."

"Who's teaching who here?" I asked.

"Just what I need, a smart-ass student. Want to go another round?"

I could hear my pager vibrating.

"Lesson two will have to wait. The office is telling me I've spent enough time with my first customer."

My first customer.

I wondered how this new portfolio of skills might serve me. How could I focus this new awareness to make a difference in people's lives? The seed of an idea germinated in my mind. For the first time in my life, I felt a purpose emerging.

Ellen loosened her embrace and let me go, laughing at the distended condom that still clung to me.

"Tell you what. I'll call the office and buy you time for a shower."

I caressed her cheek. "Naw. They never get angry until the third text. But I do have to get going."

I realized then that I was covered with more than liquid remnants of our sexual tryst. I was as sweat-drenched as if I had run a marathon.

I could hear Ellen cleaning up as the shower's warm cascades refreshed me. "Do you fuck all your customers?" she asked. Her tone was confident, playful, defiant.

"Only those who blackmail me."

She was sitting on the counter, drooling over my wet body, when I emerged. Her face became serious. " You helped me

unload a lot of resentment and grief today. For the first time in forever, I'm feeling empowered, too. Thank you for helping me find the key to unlock the bars of my self-imposed prison."

I would have taken her back to bed then and there. But there was work to do, Ellen was ten years my senior, and she was navigating extraordinary circumstances. I didn't like taking advantage of someone with impaired judgment.

"The reality is I've never had sex with a customer, Ellen. And I've spent so much time just trying to survive in this crazy world that romance has been nothing more than a pipe dream. You opened my heart to the possibilities today. Thank you for that."

Ellen Corbin pinched my ass. "I can promise you one thing, David. From now on, whenever this customer calls, she will request a certain repair professional by name."

I scribbled Kyle McClellan's name and number on my business card. "Give this guy a call. He's a lawyer I know and may be able to help you and Elise."

As I returned to my truck, I discovered a one-hundred-dollar bill in my pants pocket.

I was unprepared for what would happen when that next call came.

2

MR. WRONG

ELLEN

If this is Adam, give me the serpent.

His rented condo smelled of dirty socks and stale food. My nose told me that somewhere, there was a towel that needed washing. Dirty windows obscured an exquisite view of the State Capitol. The living room's trail of printed documents, wrinkled clothing, and half-eaten packages of Chinese food did nothing to increase my confidence about my first foray into the dating world.

It sucked. Either they are too old, divorced for a good reason, or have kids and don't want another. Or they are too needy, too controlling, too distant.

Adam epitomized them all. The sex was all about him. Not even the courtesy of a shower before or after. The scent I found stimulating at dinner morphed into revulsion as he snored like a chainsaw next to me in the rented bed in the rented condo where he lived until his divorce went through.

It was like being with Brad all over again

I dressed in the living room and got the hell out.

I was thirty-three, for Christ's sake. I was in my sexual prime. The pheromones I was radiating should be attracting men like bees to honey. But the ones I got were the drones, the creeps, or guys who still need a mommy.

I wished there were someone out there like the young man who "fixed my cable." That had become the code phrase for building my self-confidence while making me come like a bullet train.

I couldn't stop thinking about David. It had been a month since our encounter. What had happened that morning had transformed me.

I morphed from this frightened, helpless girl into a warrior woman, determined to do whatever it took to provide for my daughter and find happiness. A partner to share the journey was part of that definition. So far, I was coming up with duds.

David was so mature for his age. I bet it was because he had endured some bad things in the foster homes where he had grown up. His short verbal biography tantalized me. The intensity of his passion gave me the sense of some deeply rooted pain that still lingered there.

I couldn't imagine losing my parents when I was just starting to form my adult identity. Somehow, he had come through it without becoming a drug addict or an alcoholic. I wanted to get to know him better.

And the condom thing was so sweet. I was so glad David had thought about it because I was still in that time after giving birth where just looking at a man would have gotten me pregnant again. My hormones were driving what could have been a terrible decision. I was so glad David was watching out for me.

Adam sure didn't give a damn. He tried to tell me he didn't have any condoms while peeling off my clothes like a hungry ape holding a banana. Luckily for him, I did.

Gotta keep putting myself out there. Adam wasn't "the one." Perhaps the next guy would be.

Was it wrong to still be fantasizing about someone ten years younger? If he were here, I would fuck him until neither one of us could walk. Does that make me a cougar, a pervert, or just someone as needy as the loser men who chase me?

Adam was off of the list. "One and done," as they say. I was nothing more than a blow-up doll, something to fold up and hide from his friends when he was done. It was a role I had played for my soon-to-be ex-husband, too.

Brad and I had gotten married for all the wrong reasons. He was my security, the rich guy my parents hoped I would choose. I was his eye candy, a piece of human jewelry to put on in public, something he ignored unless it went with his ensemble.

I wondered how many other glittery items I didn't know about that might be in his jewelry box.

It was around eleven that night when I got back to the house and paid off the babysitter. I needed a good night's sleep. The next day I had an early meeting with the attorney David had suggested. Apparently, this guy had found something that might give me some leverage in the divorce. And then I'd see this new finance person Mr. McClellan recommended. He told me she was really good.

I hoped so. With a baby and zero money, I needed all the help I could get.

I was going to dream about ways to get David out there again. My hummingbird is twitching, and I wanted him to help make it sing.

✣ 3 ✣

A RETURN ENGAGEMENT

DAVID
My extraordinary experience with Ellen kept returning to my thoughts in the months that followed. Mr. McClellan had left me a cryptic note saying that she was going to be all right. "Thanks for the chance to take a swing at Brad before he took a swing at me," was how he ended the message.

Between work and trying to knock out the last of my coursework before graduation, I didn't have much time for a social life. But my dreams replayed our happenstance meeting and how Ellen Corbin had altered my understanding of sexuality.

The girls in my classes were no longer filtered by rose-colored glasses. What were once targets of physical conquest became fascinating psychological puzzles. The human mind was much more complicated and unpredictable than I imagined. When I genuinely wanted the best for someone else, karma reflected right back at me. I found that my casual conversations changed, although I didn't yet fully understand what was different about my approach.

It started with Tammy. We shared an economics class. So much of that stuff is theory and guesswork, based on history repeating itself. It was hard to grasp if for an economist, let alone a college student.

Tammy was struggling. That much was clear by the questions she asked. And our professor was one of these sanctimonious pricks who loved to express his power over us young dummies. She went up to him after class to ask a question, and he blew her off. "See me during office hours like everyone else."

"Hey, Doc," I said, sliding beside her as he packed up his stuff. "You base the supply and demand thing on vendors pleasing customers. It doesn't matter how smart the CEO is if he can't convince the customer of the value of his product, he's failed..." I took a deep breath. "And you're failing."

The professor froze. He shot me an icy stare. "What kind of entitlement gives you the right to talk to me like that?"

"Tammy and I are your customers, *sir*." I over-emphasized the word just to piss him off. "I know that academic tenure protects mediocrity and that you would rather do research than teach. If you've lost your classroom mojo, tell the dean you don't want to teach and get the hell out. And if you're uncomfortable with the way I'm speaking with you, sir, know that your attitude toward Tammy and the rest of the class gives us that same feeling." I lowered my voice. The remaining kids in the classroom were paying attention. "The difference is, at least one of us isn't afraid of you."

The professor sniffed. I didn't think anyone had ever stood up to him before. And where had that speech I spewed come from? I tried to display confidence I didn't feel. He had a lot more power and could stand in the way of my getting a diploma. But a lifelong disdain for bullies clouded my judgment. It focused me on making sure he knew it.

The man's expression softened. His sober features cleaved into an inquisitive smile. "Is this your girlfriend?"

I shook my head.

"Why do you care?"

"Once upon a time, someone cared enough about me to intervene and change my life. You inspire hundreds of students each semester with your knowledge and experience." I touched Tammy's shoulder. "Here's one who wants to learn. That, alone, should make you want to help her."

"Okay, cowboy," our professor said. He took in the stares of the few students who had witnessed our exchange. "It's easy to forget that we all owe a debt to somebody for our good fortune. Thanks for reminding me why I teach." He opened his valise and took out his lecture notes. "Let's all learn from one another. I'll hang around and answer any questions you have, and we'll stay with it until you're satisfied with the answers. And this young lady," he pointed to Tammy, "gets to go first."

Tammy gave me "the look." Her eyebrows raised. She moistened her lips, thrusting her shoulders back, subconsciously highlighting her chest. No words were spoken between us. But I knew exactly what she was saying. "Thank you," she mouthed. "Do I have your cell number?"

Before Ellen, I was just one in a shiver of sharks, circling prey. Now I was the object of interest. My female classmates were paying attention to me, perhaps because I was paying attention to them. Hips would casually brush against me, wrapped in seductive, encouraging words.

I wished I had time to take advantage of the situation.

I wanted to tell Ellen about my transformation, but she had moved out of that small house soon after our encounter, and I had lost track of her. It had been almost seven months since that day. I was beginning to think our meeting was a one-time miracle —serendipity.

The week before commencement, I got a call from financial aid. Like many students, I had amassed a ton of debt, despite working my ass off and living like a monk. When I recognized the caller ID, I thought for sure it was nearing time to pay the piper.

"Someone has paid off your account," the loan officer told me. "Congratulations. You will graduate debt-free."

I was stunned. There must have been some mistake. The loan officer assured me that there were no errors, and the situation was genuine. I wanted to know who my benefactor was but was told the person preferred to keep it confidential.

Graduation was a bittersweet day, another time when I realized how much I missed having a family. As an only child, my parents made every special occasion a holiday. Since the three of us had no genetic relatives, we populated our family with fascinating people from my parents' portfolio of friends.

"We have two families," my dad used to tell me. "We don't get to choose the cards biology deals us. But we can hand-pick our own second family. Over a lifetime, they become just as important as blood."

Vivid memories of laughter, rich conversations, and appreciation sustained me through a long series of foster homes where we rarely got past survival skills.

I thought about inviting Elliot, my last foster father and the man who had pressed me toward college. He had lost his wife to cancer the year I had graduated from high school. I was afraid that the experience of watching one of his many "sons" walk across the stage would trigger his grief.

Friends included me in their celebrations, but it just didn't feel the same. I was glad to have achieved my goal of earning a degree. But now, the real world loomed large. I still didn't have an inkling of what to do with my life. There was an emptiness in my soul, and I now needed to focus on filling it.

On the first Friday after I was free from the paper chase, my supervisor left a note in my locker. *Special request. Last job of the day. After 5 p.m.*

The address didn't register, but the neighborhood did. It was one of our city's most affluent, where the houses' minimum square footage was in the 5000s.

Thinking this might be someone who knew our general manager, I stopped by my apartment to shower and put on a freshly pressed uniform. I wanted to make a good impression for the company that was still my sole source of income.

I pulled into the driveway of a luxuriously appointed home at 5:15 on the dot and rang the bell.

I nearly fainted when Ellen answered the door.

She was a vision of joy and self-assurance. Her eyes were bright with promise and her skin a sun-drenched bronze. Her body reflected a fitness trainer's attention to detail, clad in spandex workout shorts and a sports bra. The expensive diamond tennis bracelet on her right wrist told me she had done well in the divorce. The broad smile and the radiated happiness were the complete opposite of the dejected expression I'd seen when we'd first met.

She threw her arms around me as I stood, stupefied, trying to understand what was happening.

"David! I'm so glad to see you again. Come on in and check out my new place."

It was huge, boasting a pool and a waterfall jacuzzi in the fenced backyard. Ellen told me how she learned that her husband had been seeing another woman for more than a year. When Mr. McLellan tossed that bit of information at her ex, he was suddenly quite generous, giving her half of his substantial fortune and a monthly alimony check that allowed her the freedom to be a full-time stay-at-home mom.

As she finished the tale, she put her hands on my shoulders. Her expression became serious.

"You made this all possible, David. You renewed my confidence and gave me the courage to fight for what Elise and I deserved." She leaned close to me; our foreheads touched. "I'll never be able to thank you enough for that gift. I knew deep in my heart that I had the strength and self-worth, but you helped me to unlock it."

She gave me another memorable kiss, a gentle, luxurious caress that would become the standard of comparison for years to come.

"Thank you for helping to empower me to get my life back."

I stumbled for what to say.

Ellen thoroughly enjoyed my discomfort.

"The smart guy at a loss for words. Gotta make a memory of that one."

The giggles that began as she sensed my confusion expanded into an attractive, playful laugh.

"I know what you're thinking. What does this woman want from me? Nothing at all, David. You will someday find your soulmate, and that girl will be the luckiest woman in the world. I just want you to know that I will always look out for you. And—" she flicked her eyebrows up and down seductively —"I will continue to teach you how to properly please a girl so that when that soulmate appears, you will leave her breathless and satisfied beyond her wildest dreams."

The flood of conflicting emotions I felt that first day came rushing back. It took a moment for me to find my footing. "One morning of ecstasy and I have a friend for life?"

"You felt it, too, and you know it," she said, nuzzling my nose. "Sometimes, that's how it works. Our lives can change in an instant. The smart ones have the sense to realize it."

"So there's nothing wrong with your cable?"

Ellen embraced me with another jubilant laugh.

"Someday, you'll understand the extent of your powers, my love. If you'll let me, perhaps I can help you see them."

"My love?"

Ellen punched my shoulder. "Get used to it! It's my house, my nomenclature."

I decided to change the subject.

"How is Elise? She must be, what? Ten months old by now?"

"Old enough to be spending the weekend with my parents. It's amazing how quickly I went from idiot to brilliant when they realized their wayward daughter was now a zillionaire. I bought them a house about two miles from here. They love grandparenthood."

There was more to tell, but the doorbell rang.

Ellen clapped her hands together.

"Perfect timing. There's someone I want you to meet."

☙❧

THE WOMAN WHO JOINED US APPEARED A BIT YOUNGER THAN Ellen. I guessed thirty-three. She was fit, perhaps a little heavier, but her carefully appointed business attire hid what some might have judged as imperfections.

"Meet Adrian Holloway."

I offered my hand. But Adrian embraced me in a powerful hug, kissing me on the cheek.

She pulled her head back to look me over.

"Naw. This cheek stuff just won't do."

With that, she attacked my mouth.

It differed from Ellen's kiss, more physical and controlling. I didn't resist kissing her back, emulating her style as best as I could.

She released me and leaned against the front door, panting.

"You weren't bullshitting me, Ellen. He's the real deal."

Ellen was giddy, rubbing her hands together as if something inappropriate was on her mind. She invited us into the expansive family room with a broad view of the miniature water park in her backyard.

She produced a platter of drinks, a concoction I didn't recognize.

Adrian seemed to know it well.

"Ahh! Nothing takes the edge off of a long week like a nutcracker."

I knew a thing or two about tending bar, but this was out of my league. "You two have just outstripped my knowledge of mixology. I've never heard of a nutcracker."

Ellen set a pitcher of the mixture onto the shiny coffee table at the center of the long, L-shaped sectional couch, where the three of us relaxed. "It's a New York thing, created by the owner of Flor de Mayo, a Peruvian-Chinese restaurant on the Upper West Side. The formula has had many iterations since, but the bottom line is that it's a lot like us—sweet, sexy, and dangerous."

I took a sip. Ellen was right. There was just enough fruit flavor to make me think I could chug the thing. Whatever alcohol was part of the mix was potent.

Adrian downed her glass as if it were orange juice, reaching for the pitcher for a refill. Ellen followed suit.

Well, I thought, when in Rome... I finished my own, and my hostess refilled my glass.

Ellen radiated a warm glow. She was even more attractive than I remembered.

"I wanted you to meet Adrian because a man of the world needs to learn about money. She's a senior client specialist at Sandia Wealth Advisers, and I've selected her to manage your portfolio."

"My portfolio comprises about five thousand dollars in cash, offset by about fifteen grand in credit card debt," I said, sensing a tiny slur in my speech. "What I really need is to find a better gig to pay some of it off."

Adrian finished her second nutcracker and motioned to Ellen for another refill. "Oh, you're in a much better financial position than that, my friend. And I intend to ensure that you never go hungry." She rubbed my thigh. It was not an unpleasant experience.

She executed a chomping motion with her mouth that made me wonder if she was the hungry one.

I tried to ignore the move and shared my good fortune. "This has been my lucky week. The loan officer at the financial aid office told me someone paid off my student loans. I wonder if I have a relative I didn't know about?"

Adrian spat out a mouthful of her drink, convulsing in laughter. She shook the glass, and Ellen topped it off.

"David, my boy," she said, lifting her cocktail in Ellen's direction, "meet your long-lost relative. This incestuous behavior has to stop, you two."

By now, I had lost count of how many nutcrackers I had ingested. I didn't comprehend what Adrian had just said.

Ellen beamed. "That was me. I wanted you to start your life with some resources. The long-lost relative thing was just misdirection. Those guys couldn't care less who writes the checks as long as they clear."

What she said next blew my mind. "There's an account in your name at Sandia with $400,000 in it."

Once again, my head spun. I realized that the alcohol content in the cocktails was part of it. But in an instant, my world was different. I was debt-free. I had a nest egg. And I sat between two stunning women who looked like they were about to devour me.

Ellen's eyes caught sight of what was going on inside my pants. Those eyes twinkled with delight.

"It's Adrian's job to make sure your net worth keeps 'growing,' just like something else I'm seeing."

My natural desire to maintain my self-control felt at odds with the impact of all the alcohol I had ingested. Both Ellen and Adrian had that same look the girls in my classes had been giving me for the past seven months. My eyes began to undress them as my conscience tried to suppress the lurid scenarios my libido was constructing.

My voice slurred. The room spun.

"I'm not sure I can accept your generosity, Ellen. All this kindness after just one encounter? You should be prioritizing Elise and yourself."

Ellen refilled our glasses. "Let's talk about it in the bedroom. Adrian, help me get David out of these stifling work clothes."

I chugged the concoction. The last thread of whatever self-control remained evaporated. I lusted after these beautiful women, determined to do their bidding.

I had no more recollections from that night. When my memory returned, it was the next morning, and I was in the center of Ellen's enormous bed, flanked on each side by a beautiful, soundly sleeping, naked woman.

4

MOONDANCE

ELLEN
    I had worked hard to convince myself that David wasn't the knight in shining armor young girls read about in fairy tales.

I had decided he was an affirming force of nature, empowering me to feel valued and in control of my destiny. Adrian was another kindred spirit recovering from a painful breakup. When I had told her about David, she was eager to see this amazing young man with her own eyes.

The alcohol had ripped away any restraint the three of us may have harbored. Adrian and I agreed about what we wanted to do with this gorgeous young piece of USDA Choice male meat.

He was out of that cable outfit and in his birthday suit in short order. Then we tore off our own clothes and Adrian and I guided our man to the bedroom, planting him on his back, spread-eagle in the center of my king-sized mattress.

Adrian straddled David's face, and he gave an Academy Award-winning performance. He had learned the lessons I had taught him well because Adrian was soon breathing hard. It excited me to realize that he knew a few tricks of his own, too. Adrian's every exhale included a moan that got louder the more he worked on her. Her climax was a sight to behold. Adrian's entire body shook.

She rolled off of him she came, revealing David's rock hard cock.

I opened a teakwood tea case—filled with condoms—that sat on the nightstand. I gleefully fitted him with a French tickler

I threw my legs over his shoulders in the pancake position so I could get to that expressive mouth while he fucked me. Feeling him inside rekindled the rush I felt during the first time we came together. We kissed and fucked for a good fifteen minutes straight. To have someone desire you as much as you crave them is heaven on earth. The gratitude in my heart, mixed with the perfection of his technique, guided me to one of the most emotional climaxes I can ever remember.

I wept. The dawning realization of liberation from my fear and suffering, combined with David's hunger for me, made me feel like there was no mountain I couldn't climb. My tears surprised and confused us all.

David gently touched my face with his hand, wiping a tear away with his thumb. "Are you all right?"

I could see him processing my sultry smile. "It's a girl thing. After hooking up with this portfolio of losers and all of a sudden, this guy appears who fits every dirty dream I've ever dared to dream. You're too young to be this good David. I still can't believe this is happening and I'm scared it's going to end."

David softened but the swagger was still there. "You've got to learn to live in the moment, Ellen. Your friend over there has that one figured out. You're with two people who care about you. Just let things happen."

I couldn't keep my hands off of Davids pecs. "Is that how you survived all the shit you went through?"

"Yeah. Except the 'care about you part.' I've never had that piece until now. It's one hell of an aphrodisiac."

Adrian raised a hand. "I don't need a fucking aphrodisiac. Will you guys quit trying to make sense of this and can we all get back to the bonk-fest?"

David grinned at Adrian, but I could tell he was still talking to me. "There's something else going on. It's too deep and too hard to comprehend right now. My late foster mom once told me that the difference between making love and fucking is that one begins in the heart and the other begins below the belt." He began to kiss me again, his interest rising as he worked on my mouth. "She said when the feelings are real, the sex is beyond belief."

That did it. I hovered above David and slowly lowered myself toward his waiting lips. Adrian watched, transfixed, at the end of the bed. David started moving his tongue, side to side, across the top of my quivering clit, just as I had taught him. And he added his own twist. He inserted his two middle fingers into me and began a gentle but firm hooking motion that drove me wild. David closed his lips around me and gently sucked, his tongue still spinning circles around the tip.

Minutes later, I experienced another tempestuous orgasm.

Adrian's fingers moved toward her wet pussy, and she began rubbing her pleasure center as she watched us.

Then, David's right hand encircled his cock, and he stroked it.

I took the proceedings up a notch. "Come for me," I said, encouraging them. "Come for me now. Let go and give me everything. I want to watch you come! Please. Please come for me!"

The right words always finish the sentence with a flourish. Adrian peaked first. She squealed with delight.

But it was David who blew my mind. He arched, propelling his hips into the air as his climax came over him. He undulated, and his condom quickly filled with the largest ejaculation I had ever seen. He kept pumping and pumping as his own seed seeped to the ring at the base, covering his pubic hair with a thick, white coat.

Adrian saw what was happening. Without a word, we pulled off David's protection and lapped up the evidence of his excitement together. His eyes widened when we reached the top of his cock and our mouths found one another.

Everything about me is heterosexual. But in that instant, the allure of Adrian's lips and the feeling of her tongue tangling with mine was wonderful. I knew she felt the same way because we rose from David's waist, embracing and kissing each other with abandon.

Our hands found their south, and we massaged each other's pulsating pussies.

David graciously slid out from under us. He lay sideways on the mattress to witness the spectacle, which aroused us even more.

This took me back to my same-sex experimentation in high school. We were all finding ourselves then. Girls had a better understanding of our bodies' coital geography and didn't require the coaching the boys did to get us off. I discovered having sex with a girlfriend was as much fun for my boyfriend to watch as it was for me to role-play.

Two of us had performed for the quarterback of the football team one lunch hour. The wet circle on his jeans that afternoon became the stuff of legends.

"Okay, girlfriend," I said. "Show me what you can do among the bushes. I bet I can make you come first."

Adrian was a competitor. It quickly became clear she was in this one to win. She crawled over me until we were in the full sixty-nine position and worked her magic.

The one advantage I think women have when giving each other oral sex is knowing exactly how it feels. Instinct takes over, and we can please each other without the training that men require.

We both moaned as we slurped. Our pursuit of pleasuring one another was delivering its mutual benefit. Any inhibitions we might have felt about lesbian sex went out the window as we both neared the finish line.

David's eyes widened as he took in our exhibition. He pulled off his condom and began his self-pleasuring handiwork again. "You guys should consider letting me record you two with my phone," he joked. "We could make some serious money with this."

I gave up the girl on girl challenge and said, "Oh, no, you don't!"

Adrian and I both went for his cock. I got there first and began sucking on the tip as hard as I could while pumping his shaft with my fist. Adrian put her head beneath mine and tickled his balls with her tongue. David's eyes widened. The memory of our sixty-nine competition came back to me. I slid a pair of fingers inside of Adrian, circling her passion point with my thumb.

The sight of two women totally focused on his sexual gratification was too much for David. He filled my mouth with his warm production for a second time.

My experience with men in the past was that multiple orgasms usually generated a lighter load. Not in David's case. He came like a geyser, as if he knew exactly how to accommodate my fetish for world-class oral sex.

Adrian gently pressed me away from him, taking David's erection into her mouth as he continued to shoot jets of semen, which she excitedly encouraged by gently slurping his surging head.

I watched, mesmerized, as his ejaculation seemed to renew in intensity and volume. I had seen nothing like it. It fascinated Adrian. She continued to swallow each blast, totally enjoying the experience. David's hips reflexively lifted off of the mattress. Adrian held onto his shaft with both hands, circling his head with her tongue between the powerful spurts.

When David's orgasm finally subsided, the three of us lay side by side on the bed, exhausted, satiated, and blissfully happy. Adrian and I cackled like two schoolgirls who'd raided our parents' liquor cabinet. David lay between us, shaking his head as he tried to process everything that had just happened.

"You're the one who could be a top-notch porn star," Adrian said, tickling David's ear with her tongue.

David shook his head. "Nah. The returns are better in an S&P mutual fund. And besides, I can't make the magic unless there's an attraction."

He gave Adrian one of the most tender, romantic kisses I'd ever witnessed. And when he turned his gaze to me, what I saw in his eyes made me long for another round.

David covered his nether regions with his hands. "Don't even think about it," he said. "I'm going to need a week to recover."

"You're young," I whispered, biting an earlobe with my teeth. "I'll give you eight hours."

Our sweat-drenched bodies curled into a three-way spoon, and we were all soon fast asleep.

5

ADRIAN

DAVID
It's impossible to describe the sensation of waking up between two beautiful women and not being able to remember anything about the night before.

As I strained to recall what I knew must have been one of the most memorable experiences of my young life, I determined that my drinking days were over.

"Good morning, handsome,"

Ellen murmured into my ear as she cuddled me from behind.

My arms held Adrian close in front of me. The peaceful rise and fall of their breathing, the nearly synchronized beating of their hearts, and the erotic mixture of scents that were tantalizing whispers of the night before: those were the things that became my definition of "afterglow."

I gently disengaged from Adrian and rolled over to embrace Ellen.

Ellen's expression communicated a thousand different emotions. Acceptance, gratitude, awe, excitement, and joy mixed with the pure pleasure of discovery. The tiny wrinkles at the edges of her eyes reminded me of my mother. The subtle ripple of her lips brought back memories of my first kiss with a girlfriend who knew how. But the telepathic connection was new to me. I felt whispers that first day when Ellen seemed to read my mind. It was a sixth sense that only we two could share. We had cemented a permanent bond that would go well beyond the bedroom.

In fact, we really knew very little about one another. But I thought we both sensed that something special had happened on that first day our paths had crossed. A mutual trust had quickly blossomed, and the beginnings of a deep and meaningful lifelong friendship were taking root.

I whispered, not wanting to awaken Adrian, "I remember little about last night. I hope I didn't do anything to hurt either of you."

"You took good care of us, David. And I think we took good care of you."

"I don't like not knowing. From now on, I hope you will understand if I stick to Coca-Cola so I'll be able to make a memory of the magic."

Ellen tightened her embrace. "We will have many more magic moments, my love. I will always be here for you and will support your path toward happiness, with whatever bumps come with it."

"There's that 'my love' thing again. How can you love me when we've only been together twice?"

"Go with the flow, David. Don't ask questions. Just accept what is given."

It was time for some honesty. "I guess I'm a little gun-shy, Ellen. The sting of losing my family and the conditional acceptance that had eluded me across a string of foster homes makes me a little suspicious. This is new territory. I hope you can be patient with me as I work through it."

You are special, David. I'm not asking for anything in return. My payback will be the joy of watching you grow and prosper."

Our foreheads touched in what would become a symbol of our mutual affection. It was hard to see Ellen's face because we both had tears in our eyes.

For the first time since my parents' deaths, and perhaps for the first time in Ellen's life, we began to contemplate the meaning of love.

What Ellen said next surprised me.

"You could make a living doing this."

"Doing what?"

"Building self-worth. Helping women uncover their power."

That confused me. "What do you mean?"

She lowered her voice. "Teaching them about things like self-worth, acceptance, and strength. Intimacy goes way beyond the physical. But physical attraction is a powerful elixir. It rips away our shields and can open us up to a deeper understanding of ourselves and the world."

"Are you suggesting that I get intimate with strangers?"

"They wouldn't be strangers. They would be 'clients.'"

I still didn't get it.

Ellen's eyes lit up when the idea came to her. "Let's test drive with Adrian. I wanted her to meet you because she's always had body issues and low self-esteem outside of her left-brain comfort zone. She needed those nutcrackers to let go of her inhibitions."

"That's crazy. We've just met. How am I supposed to 'fix' her?"

"Leave it to me. I'll cue you. Just let your magic flow."

I wasn't sure about this idea. The whole notion of the bedroom being a place where you re-discover your mojo was appealing. I didn't yet have the confidence to believe that I could play the role that Ellen had described.

But I decided to trust this amazing woman.

"Okay, Ellen. But I still can't see how this thing could become a profession."

"Surround yourself with good people. Tell them what you need. Give them the support to be able to be successful. And every problem will ultimately take care of itself."

Adrian's voice brought us back into the present. "Hey, you two, where's the shower? Is it big enough for three?"

It was.

Ellen's bathroom was as large as my apartment, with one of those walk-in showers where the entire ceiling was one big cascade. A few memories of the night before emerged as these two exquisite women bathed me under the gentle flow of warm raindrops.

Ellen's introduction, the implication of a recent breakup, and Adrian's business resume made me want to learn more about this energetic woman who was now my financial adviser. I could see Ellen's face in my peripheral vision as she watched me concentrate on Adrian's eyes.

My mentor nodded her head. Mouthing the words, "Please her," as she quietly slipped out of the shower, pointing to a condom in the soap dish, leaving the two of us alone.

I took hold of Adrian's hands. Her gaze rose to meet mine.

"Thank you for last night, Adrian, and for everything you've done to help me."

She tickled that part of me that did most of the work. "To say it was 'a pleasure' would be the mother of all understatements."

Here I was, twenty-one years old, standing naked in the shower with an attractive woman who had taken me to heights of sexual satisfaction that I couldn't even remember. My subconscious must have recorded some of it. I was suddenly feeling very drawn to her.

Then I said the words that would become the mantra for the rest of my life.

"How can I please you?"

Adrian was sober now. Her face darkened. The reality of her own low self-worth started to appear.

"This has been fun, David. But how could I possibly turn you on unless you were drunk? Look at me. I'm an overweight numbers nerd. What could be more unattractive?"

I frowned. "I disagree. And you haven't answered my question. How can I please you?"

"What could possibly be appealing about me? Answer me that, mister man-of-my-dreams?"

I stood back, inspecting her. She was heavier than the ideal that everyone sees on television. But I could appreciate the muscle beneath the surface. Her smile revealed attractive dimples and near-perfect teeth. And I was mesmerized by what must be inside that numbers nerd head. What could I say that might build her self-esteem?

I moved closer. "Smile. Pretend that stuck-up girl you hated in high school just walked by your desk and fell flat on her ass."

The dimples emerged.

"These," I said, rubbing them with my fingers. "Your face is tantalizing when you smile." I moved my hands down to her shoulders. "Your posture is pitch-perfect. It conveys confidence, even if you may not believe it on the inside." I cupped her generous endowments. "And do you know how many women would love to have these flawless breasts?" I grasped her hips, lightly moving them from side to side. "When you walked in the front door, the way you swayed these, the assurance in your gait—it was like a model on the runway."

I returned my hands to her head. As the warm water cascaded around them, I ran my fingers through her hair.

"This," I said. "What makes you beautiful is what's inside this incredible brain. To comprehend the calculus of wealth as you do, to grasp the meaning of equations that, to most of us, are just a row of numbers and symbols, and to help hard-working people turn their savings into fortunes—how could any man with half the brain you have, not fall in love with this awe-inspiring woman?"

I had her full attention. She had become a little girl, captivated by a magician.

"We all default to our defects. Finding fault is ingrained in that left brain that is making you financially rich. What breaks my heart is that you aren't allowing yourself to accept that it's the imperfections that make us interesting." I circled my thumb around her navel. "The little extras that make us sexy."

I brought her face within inches of my own and nuzzled her nose. "And your magnificent authenticity—that makes you so seductive."

Adrian still wasn't convinced. "Being a smart ass is authenticity?"

"The truth behind it is."

I moved my mouth close to her ear. "I can fulfill any sexual fantasy you can dream of, Adrian. But you are the one who must believe what the rest of us know—that you are a stunning, imperfect, miraculous soul, deserving of respect, admiration, and, yes, love."

I didn't know where those sentiments had come from. Before I could understand what it meant, my father told me that there was a bit of paranormal in our gene pool. My mother said that the most beautiful words flow through us and not from us. Years later, Ellen would say that this was both my gift and my curse—the ability to articulate the beauty in everything and everyone.

Tears streamed down Adrian's face, mingling with the rivulets of water from the shower.

She took my head into her hands and went after my mouth. It was as if I had unleashed a caged animal. Simply describing her aroused me, too.

Backing me into a corner against the tiles, she continued kissing me as she ripped open the condom wrapper and applied its contents, holding the tip with one hand and rolling the rubber down over my shaft. The motion made me grow and thicken with each stroke.

Adrian then turned us around so her back was against the shower wall. She guided my thickness inside of her. "Fuck me," she panted. "Fuck me so hard and long and lovely that I beg you for more. Take me, David. You've made me believe I'm beautiful. Now fuck me as if I'm the most amazing woman you've ever known."

It began as a plaintive appeal. But as Adrian said the words, her voice became stronger, more self-assured, and ultimately formidable and forceful.

I did exactly as she asked. She wrapped her arms around my neck and her legs around my waist, urging me to slam her back against the tiles until it felt like we might shatter the drywall behind them. Adrian threw back her head with a look I recognized in Ellen as she found her strength. Triumph emanated from her face as she let her arms slacken to receive my hammering thrusts.

As she neared climax, her hips tightened. She was nodding now, directing me. "Good," she said. "More. More. Harder. Almost there."

Suddenly she peaked. Her arms splayed against the shower walls. Her entire body trembled as an orgasm overtook her.

Adrian spoke between gulps of air to the unseen presence we both knew was waiting outside of the shower. "Ellen? If you ever let this guy go, I'll be grabbing him and won't ever give him back."

6

PILLOW TALK

ELLEN
     It took less than a minute. Adrian had barely pulled out of the driveway and my cell rang.

"Oh my God, Ellen. You discovered a five-star prospect."

"And you, my friend, are making it possible for us to develop him."

"Seriously, Ellen. What he said about self-confidence and beauty? I've wanted to believe that all my life. I never could, until today. Money can't buy love, but if David had hourly rates, I would be a regular."

My idea was taking shape. "I want to talk more about that. We still don't know David well enough to have confidence that he can keep professional boundaries."

"Way ahead of you, girlfriend," Adrian said. "I think I can come up with an enticing grad school package. And I know who we should give him as client number one."

◈

ALONE AGAIN, DAVID AND I SPOONED TOGETHER IN BED.

None of the boys I knew in school had David's depth of compassion and empathy. Few men did. There we were, two people a decade apart in age, lying naked next to one another, talking as if we were lifelong friends.

And the test drive with Adrian had convinced me that David's skills were sellable. What if he truly could help other women like he had helped Adrian and me? Did I care if sex with them were part of the process? Nope. Just as long as he "saved the last dance for me."

I wrapped a hand around the object of my affection. I could feel it thickening, the warmth of his breath caressing my hair, his fingers lightly circling the tips of my nipples. I selected some protection from the teakwood box and applied it by feel, my hands working behind my back as David continued to accommodate me.

I rolled on top, guiding him into me. My grinding was gentler this time.

I kissed the top of his head, losing my face in his hair, thoroughly enjoying every tantalizing touch.

My desire grew. I tipped his chin upward so our mouths could meet. David's kisses were much more tender than passionate—slow, delicious, and loving. He was now a full participant in the friction we made.

"You are an amazing lover, David Orion."

"And you are an extraordinary woman," he whispered between kisses. "I feel so lucky that I am beginning to know the heart that beats inside of your beautiful body. That is the true source of my arousal."

"Do you sweet talk all the girls like that?"

"Hey! That was from the heart. Are you trying to destroy the mood?"

I did not want to destroy the mood. I increased the pace of my grind. "No, my love. I just find it hard to accept compliments, especially when they are put so poetically."

David circled my nipple with his tongue. "We'll have to work on that. And can you find something else besides 'my love?' It's too soon for that language."

I pressed a breast against his lips. Damn, it felt good. "It's what I feel, you ding dong. Let me have my moment."

"Infatuation leaps into bloom," he said, licking his way over the top of my rounded flesh and toward my neck. "Love takes time."

I shuddered when he found another erogenous zone I didn't know existed. "Where did you get that wisdom?"

David felt my tremor and nibbled the spot. "The wisest romance coach on the planet. Dear Abbey."

I put a hand on each side of his face, pulling his mouth to meet mine. "Dear Abbey is dead."

"Her wisdom," David said, arching up into me as he accepted my oral probing, "is timeless. You are a terrific woman, an exquisite lover, and a priceless spirit. Now shut up and fuck me."

God, how that turned me on. I knew that behind the sarcasm, he meant it. It wasn't just a line to control me. It was a genuine expression of affection, and again, it took me to the heights of orgasm.

After my climax, I desperately wanted David to follow. But he surprised me.

"Let me help you come, too," I said.

David's warmth radiated maturity beyond his years.

"No, Ellen. My primary joy comes from pleasing you."

He circled the tip of my nose with his finger.

"If this love thing is going to work, I want to get to know every-thing about you that makes you the exceptional woman you are. Pleasing you goes way beyond our physical attraction. Most of the women I've dated have bailed on me at the first sign of a storm. I want to dance with you in the rain. I want to understand the emotions behind your tears and the fuel that fires your joy. Most of all, I want to understand your mind. Intellect is so sexy to me. When I connect with what's going on inside that beautiful head of yours, that's when the real magic happens."

I wanted to ravish him all over again. There was more.

"I know that part of my attraction to you is the fact that my own mother isn't around."

"So I'm a mother figure?"

"That's for the shrinks to establish," he said, a sly grin creasing his face. "If we're going to be a thing, Elise has to be part of the picture, too. I'm determined for your miracle girl to know what it's like to have an attentive, loving male figure in her life for as long as our relationship lasts. But you're the boss. Please tell me if I ever overstep my bounds."

Words couldn't express how all that made me feel.

My heart was bursting with happiness and gratitude at that moment. I was so at peace when I was with David. Despite the difference in our ages, I could feel myself falling in love.

And yet, I fought it with every fiber of my being. He was right. We were still getting to know one another. And David deserved a soul mate from his own generation. So, I reasoned, did I.

Why, I wondered to myself, couldn't a man closer to my own age have this combination of a giving heart and an olympian's skills in the bedroom?

I had survived a painful divorce by living moment to moment. I decided that, where David was concerned, I would take things as they came.

❧ 7 ❧

MONICA

DAVID

Two weeks had passed, and it still felt like I was recovering from my experience with Ellen and Adrian. From a career perspective, I had a BA in Business Administration diploma hanging on the wall in my apartment, but no idea what I wanted to do with it.

I was also wrestling with my feelings for this amazing woman who had changed my life. Our relationship was unique. A therapist might conclude that we were codependent. Ellen was an alchemy of mother, sister, and girlfriend—elements that spun a confusing web of emotions. I wasn't sure what I was to her. Perhaps protégé was an appropriate description, although "sexual plaything" was definitely a powerful part of the mix.

And then there was Adrian. She was the first to experience my intentioned desire to build self-esteem and confidence. Today I would see if I had truly made any difference.

Sandia Wealth Advisers was the anchor tenant in one of the larger buildings downtown. Adrian beamed at me from behind her immense desk. Two large monitors scrolled stock market data and portfolio information as she tapped a keyboard that she quietly slid out of sight when she stood to greet me.

Her embrace was warm and sensitive, not the bear hug I remembered from our first meeting. She ushered me to a pair of enormous leather chairs, positioned to take advantage of the view of the city outside of the floor-to-ceiling windows.

Adrian leaned forward, arms folded, a sly smile morphed her face, topped off with a conspiratorial wink.

"How are you?"

"Still processing everything."

"Ellen didn't tell me you were a biz major. That's another delicious dimension."

"True. I kind of fell into it, but I'm not sure what to do with it."

"So, you're like most kids, fresh out of school and still not sure what you want to be when you grow up?"

"That pretty much describes it."

"Hmm." I could see the wheels turning in Adrian's brain. "I'll go over your holdings with you in a minute. Would you like some advice?"

"Of course. You are one of the smartest women I know."

Adrian laughed. "Just in the left brain, David. You still have a few things to help me reinforce in that part of my mind where my elusive self-worth is still trying to hide from me."

Adrian stroked her chin with her thumb and index finger. I would learn that this was a sign that her mind was at work.

"I'm a one-dimensional person, David, probably a little too focused on the money stuff. But too few people really understand the formula for building wealth. If you're still trying to figure out what to do with your life, perhaps learning the ins and outs of finance might be a pleasant distraction."

I was trying to follow her. "Are you suggesting grad school?"

"Yes. An MBA and an internship while you're working on it. We have to get you out of pickup trucks and into a BMW."

The thought of continuing my education was on my mind. Like several friends, I took the GRE as a backstop in case I couldn't find a job.

Adrian handed me a manila folder.

"Take that home and let it marinate for a few days. Then let me know what you think."

I read the contents. It was an internship agreement and a scholarship application.

Adrian could see the confusion in my eyes.

"It's a job offer and a meal ticket for grad school, silly. I'm offering to hire you and cover the bulk of your educational expenses. Sandia has a great program to identify and nurture high-potential students. If there were ever someone who fit the bill, David, it's you. If you work your ass off, you can finish in a year. But if I were you, I'd take the full two-year time frame that comes with the deal. That should give you the capacity to find yourself and—" a devilish look came over Adrian's face—"enjoy the ride."

There was a knock. I turned to see a tall, well-dressed man standing in Adrian's office doorway.

"Still up for dinner tonight?"

Adrian nodded. "I'll be ready at six."

The man winked at her, his self-assured smile morphing into concern as he saw me.

"He's a client, Lance. Just remember that there's very little competition on the extra mile."

He dismissed me and pointed a finger at her, popping his thumb as if it were a pistol.

"I'm pretty good on the extra mile. See you at six."

She watched his well-built form as he turned and walked down the hallway.

I raised my eyebrows. "Well. That didn't take long."

Adrian feigned ignorance. "What are you talking about?"

"Our conversation in Ellen's rain forest. Amazing what a little belief in yourself can do."

Adrian's eyes shifted toward my belt line. "We'll see if he can measure up."

She stood. "Want to see how rich you are?"

"Sure."

We were moving in the direction of her desk when Adrian seemed to remember something.

"Oh, by the way. I have someone I need you to meet."

ॐ

THE SUNSET PAINTED AN ORANGE GLOW ON THE EDGES OF THE evening clouds as I took the elevator up to the twenty-third floor of the Haden Condominiums. To the uninitiated, this didn't seem like the place where a twenty-eight-year-old finance intern would live. Monica wasn't just any twenty-eight-year-old.

The building bore her last name.

Adrian had briefed me on her backstory. The daughter of one of the country's richest men, Monica Haden had dutifully followed daddy's instructions, earning a finance degree, joining the most exclusive sorority, and doing everything a good girl should. When he had spoken to the CEO of Sandia Wealth Advisers, Monica had jumped to the top of the internship list, earning her MBA in twelve months and continuing with the firm thereafter.

I was still uncertain about all of this, but Ellen had just two words when I told her about my first appointment, "Please her."

Adrian's assessment was succinct. Monica was miserable. She didn't like the work. She had hated her gold-plated university experience. She felt trapped in a life that her father was guiding with Svengali precision.

I knew people like that at school. They usually rebelled, transferring their anger for others to the nearest nice-guy who will put up with it. I had an uneasy premonition as I rang the condo doorbell.

What greeted me was absolute perfection.

She was about five feet, seven inches tall, one hundred twenty pounds tops. The city's best orthodontist had likely carefully arranged the teeth she revealed behind a thin smile. Chocolate-brown eyes and dark eyelashes that looked to be the real deal offset long, blond hair. Her skill with mascara and makeup was obviously well-honed. What seemed out of place was the size of her chest. I assumed Daddy had paid for a significant enhancement.

She appeared to still be in her work clothes—a gray, pinstriped suit coat combination that covered a white collared blouse. I guessed that she had unbuttoned it for my benefit, well below what human resources probably allowed.

Monica studied me, slight eyebrow movements up or down, judging the nuances of what she saw.

After a moment, she found her manners.

"David," she said with a practiced upward turn at the corners of her mouth. "Ms. Holloway has told me a lot about you. Come in."

The condo was stunning. A continuous bay of picture windows framed the evening cityscape beyond. Expensive original artwork by John Curren, Mark Bradford, and Damien Hirst adorned the walls. I imagined an interior decorator arranged the furniture with a careful feng shui touch to maximize the view's power.

Was there anything about this girl's world that was real?

Monica opened the doors to an oak credenza, revealing a line of top-shelf liquors.

"What are you drinking?"

"Just a Coke if you have it, please."

"Ahh. He speaks. I hope you don't mind if I imbibe."

I moved toward the cabinet. "Allow me. What's your pleasure?"

Her eyebrows raised in what seemed like approval.

"A lemon drop martini. You might as well use the big shaker and make four at once. It's been one of those days."

I arranged the ingredients on the granite-topped island in the center of the kitchen area and beckoned to her.

"Pull up a bar stool, Monica, and tell me about life."

"Living the dream." Her face revealed a combination of emotions that gave the phrase a different meaning. Resignation, sadness, and seething anger. "Best education money can buy. World travel. A great job. Attentive friends who envy me." She swept an arm to encompass the condo and all its accouterments. "I want for nothing."

She watched as I squeezed the last of the fresh lemons into the shaker, filled it with ice, and begin mixing.

I popped the key question on my mind.

"How do you like following the path that your father has so kindly mapped out for you?"

"I'll answer that after I'm properly medicated. Stop shaking and pour."

Monica produced a tumbler so big that it could hold the shaker's entire contents.

"Would you like sugar on the rim?"

"Just pour, David. I suppose it's okay to call you David since you're younger than me, although it sounds like you are Ms. Holloway's chosen one already."

I poured.

She drank, draining two-thirds of the martini in a single pull.

"Make me another just like this and then, come. Sit."

Monica left me to my duties and threw her suit coat onto the counter, popping open another button on her blouse. She removed the conservative bra that framed her chest in a way that minimized the staring at the office. She plopped down in a corner of a leather sectional couch that surrounded a banzai tree on top of a clear glass coffee table.

Monica took a more moderate dose of her lemon drop and shook her head.

"I hate these goddamn banzai trees."

I tried changing the subject.

"The view from up here is spectacular."

"That's exactly what Daddy said the day he gave me the keys. I had never even been in here before then."

The entire condo had a cold, abstract vibe, a set of building blocks you could buy already assembled into a spacecraft or a transforming truck. I wondered what Monica might create if she took these fully envisioned things down to their smallest essence and started from scratch.

"So, this doesn't reflect your personal style?"

"Nothing about my life reflects my personal style. I'm guessing that's why Adrian—Ms. Holloway—sent you to me. You're too young to be a shrink. I've been to a half dozen of those, and they all tell me my addiction has to do with the divorce."

"Divorce?"

"My parents split when I was nine. Why do psychiatrists always assume everything has to do with your parents?"

I put the shaker down onto the coffee table within Monica's reach. I sat on the opposite end of the sofa, keeping my distance.

"Something tells me your mom isn't the problem."

She beckoned me, wiggling a finger.

"Something tells me proximity is your problem. Get your ass over here next to me so I can smell you."

Monica downed the last of her first serving and re-filled her glass. I moved closer, sitting about three feet away from her at the corner of the couch.

"If you've been in therapy, they probably have asked you how you rebel. It doesn't take a Ph.D. to understand that this is about your dad."

Monica shook her head. She looked disappointed in my performance so far.

"Bingo, Einstein. His hands have been around my throat ever since he got custody. I hate him. But I hate the idea of being poor even more."

"We can talk about that. But right now, I'm interested in how you are trying to hurt him."

Her eyes showed zero emotion as she answered me.

"I fuck everything that walks. He knows I do it. Had an IUD put in to keep me from giving him a baby that wasn't the appropriate pedigree. My sexual activity is the one thing he's too scared to nail me about, so I plunge the knife in every chance I get."

"When did this start?"

"When I was thirteen. Right around the time that I got my first period."

She put her hands under her breasts and shook them.

"Demanded these as an eighteenth birthday present and got some bigger ones on my own at twenty-one. It hooks the boys like bees to honey."

She took another long drink. The liquor was starting to work. Her eyelids drooped. Her mouth bent into a half-smile. The hurt that wouldn't go away was dulled for the moment. Monica's eyes darted up and down my body. She was sizing me up as her next conquest.

"It doesn't sound like it's helped," I said. "Guys with one-track minds become boring when you exhaust the meager contents of their mind palace."

I wanted to know what kept Monica going. It couldn't just be the hate.

"If you could have your dreams come true," I said, "what would they be?"

That triggered Monica. She jumped off the couch and started pacing back and forth in front of the long wall of windows.

"Now you are talking like my shrink again. Why do you think Adrian sent you to me? Something happened to her after she was with you; I know that part. She was instantly a different woman, and now she's getting laid. But I can fuck anyone I want, so unless she thinks you can take me to the moon and back in the bedroom, there must be something else."

I wasn't sure why I was here. Did Adrian think I could say a few words and untangle seventeen years of anger? I tried a variation on my magic words.

"What would make you happy?"

Monica put down her tumbler and climbed into my lap, undoing another button on her blouse and thrusting her chest at my face.

"Fuck me. I like younger guys."

"Wait a minute, Monica. I'm not sure that doing that will make you happy."

"I'll pay you if that's what you want. You're fresh out of school and probably mired in debt. Perhaps a thousand dollars would take a little chunk out of it."

I lifted her up and put her back in her corner.

"Everything I do is to help people heal. Having sex with you in this state will not contribute to that."

Monica's disbelief morphed into rage. I got the sense she was rarely rejected.

"Nobody tells me 'no.'" She was confused, angry, and drunk. She ripped open the rest of the buttons on her blouse, peeling it off to reveal her substantial wares. "Are you going to fuck me or not?"

I stood up and started for the door.

"I'll be glad to help you take back your power, Monica. Maybe at some point, sex will be part of that. But not when you're drunk and not to help you hurt your father."

Monica ran after me and seized my arm.

"Don't you see how much he's hurt me? I don't know what a normal childhood is like. I never even had a job until he got me one at Sandia. I don't know if I could survive if he cut off the money. Don't you get that?"

I turned to face her, shaking her grip loose and grasping her arms. I was tired and angry, too. I was angry at Monica's father for clipping her wings but angrier at her for not directing her fury toward securing her freedom.

"Listen to me, woman. You have used your considerable powers already, but not toward a positive outcome. What at first must have dulled the sadness that surrounded you when your parents split has become an anger-management addiction. What do you feel after you've had your way with these guys? Do you even climax?"

"You're getting pretty personal for someone I barely know."

"Answer the fucking question, Monica. What happens in bed?"

"I feel a sense of victory when I make them come. Their spurts against my cervix are my empowerment. I've caused them to give me everything they have."

"And you're not using any protection?"

"Don't be prudish with me, David. The risk is part of the excitement. Yes, I get checked regularly. No STDs."

I wanted to shake her, but I didn't.

"Listen to yourself, Monica. All you are doing is prolonging the pain. Yes, your father is hurting, but it's because he doesn't know how to help you. Guys like him had to fight for every penny. That he tried to protect you is admirable. He just went about it the wrong way."

Her temper flared. Her face was red hot. Her breaths became

shorter. Her fists were so tight that they shook. "You're on his side. I've heard all that shit in therapy. I don't buy a word of it."

I could see a light on in what I assumed was a mammoth master bedroom and pushed her in that direction. It was time for her to sleep this off.

Monica batted my hands away. Her sneer reflected a cornered animal. But she was cooperating, backing toward the bedroom like a predator luring its prey.

"Believe it, Monica. Your dad loves you. He just doesn't know how to show it the right way. Direct some of that selfishness toward helping him learn what you really need. You've got his fiery blood running through your veins. Use it to free yourself to be who you are."

The bedroom was gargantuan, floor-to-ceiling blinds discretely hiding whatever might go on inside from outside eyes. A king-sized oak poster bed was the center of attention. New-age music whispered a backdrop.

Monica was triumphant. Yet her voice echoed disappointment. Perhaps I was like the others after all; another shallow man searching for a new, shiny object.

"You're going to fuck me, like all the rest, aren't you, David?"

I loosened my grip on her arms, gently depositing her on the edge of the bed.

"No, Monica. We'll do things my way or not at all."

"Now you sound like Daddy."

I shook my head. "There's a difference. The choice of whether we do this together is yours."

She was silent for a moment, trying to comprehend what I had said. I worried that the time might still not be right since she had consumed so much alcohol. But she had built up a tolerance. There was no slur in her voice. I hoped the repression that the vodka softened might also thaw some ice around her heart.

"I'm interested," she finally said. "I haven't had an orgasm in ten years. If you can do that, my thousand-dollar offer stands."

I shook my head and turned again to leave.

"I can't help you, Monica. Yes, you are attractive, even without the plastic tits. And you're smart. Your work at Sandia impresses everyone, even though you hate it. And while you might not afford a place like this, with your brains and the drive you got from your father's gene pool, you could likely build a bigger fortune than he has.

"I challenge you to think about something besides the money. What would happiness look like if you could have it your way? You've lived under his control for so long it might be hard to find role models who can teach you the things your father can't, like nurturing and mutual respect and wanting the best for the other person. I think in his heart of hearts, your dad wants to give you these gifts along with wings to fly wherever you want to go. He just doesn't know how to do it. So, you must teach him as you learn."

I faced her to drive my message home.

"Life isn't supposed to be easy. We all have to navigate the darkness. Most people can't deal with the rollercoaster and self-destruct in victimhood. That's what you're doing now, Monica. The drinking, the unsafe sex. You're slowly committing suicide. In your mind, it's the ultimate retribution."

I ran my fingers through Monica's hair. The soft strands felt cool to the touch. I imagined her without the makeup or silicone. The potential drew me to her. But perhaps tonight, the answer was keeping my distance.

"The tragedy is that you already have every tool you need to build a life, to find your own definition of happiness, and to break free of controlling men who just want to fuck a billionaire's daughter. I hurt for you, Monica. Not because of what's happened to you. But because you refuse to see that you have the power to transform yourself into the woman you truly want to become."

I was prepared to walk out of Monica's life. But then I saw something. A single tear rolled down her cheek, followed by another and another until her head fell into her hands, and she sobbed. It was an uncontrolled tsunami of grief, probably years in the making. She fell back onto the bed, emitting a primal scream, releasing her spirit animal and all the anger it harbored into the room. She rolled onto her stomach and started pounding the pillows, continuing to shriek incoherently.

I felt like I was watching a time machine of catharsis. It started with the nine-year-old who couldn't understand why her parents no longer loved one another and moved through dozens of events along the timeline of her life that reinforced her anger, sorrow, and shame. As she approached the present, her fury was almost uncontrollable. She gagged. I barely got a wastebasket under her before she vomited up the booze.

Monica rolled again onto her back, clutching her stomach. Her massive sobs subsided into whimpers.

I found a washcloth in the master bathroom, ran it under some cool water, and lay on the bed next to her, putting it on her forehead.

Monica's face was plaintive, pleading.

"Please," she said. "I don't know what love feels like."

"Give me ten minutes," I said.

⚜

MONICA WAS ON HER BACK IN THE CENTER OF HER BED WHEN I returned. Her eyes, red from crying, focused blankly on the center of the ceiling.

I ran my fingers through her hair to bring her back from whatever place her mind had taken her.

"May I undress you?"

The defiance was gone. It was a child's voice that answered me.

"What are you going to do?"

"Help you begin to heal."

She nodded, closing her eyes in resignation. There was no reason to trust me, but Monica was too emotionally depleted to resist.

I removed her clothes, carrying her in my arms in the bathroom's direction. Her eyes widened when she saw what I had done.

I had found a half-dozen votive candles, which I deployed around the room to cast soft, dancing wisps of light against the walls. There were two roses among a flower arrangement near the front door. I had peeled the petals and created a walkway toward the jacuzzi tub, which I filled with warm water and a fragrant bath bomb I had discovered in a glass container at the edge of the sink. New-age music softly sang through the speaker on my cell phone.

I lowered her into the spacious jacuzzi, resting her head and back against the side, and turned on the jets.

I sat on the floor next to the tub as the water massaged her.

"Take a deep breath," I said. "Inhale the healing energy."

She complied, her chest rising with the inhalation. I could understand how it could be a man-magnet. Her eyes were closed as her other senses drank in the atmosphere.

"Good," I continued. "Hold it for the count of four and then let it go, releasing whatever negative juju still is trying to hide inside of you."

She exhaled.

Her muscles relaxed. She sank into the warm water's welcoming embrace. Her breathing slowed. The stress lifted as we repeated the exercise for the next few minutes.

When I felt like she was a little more centered. I asked a question.

"Tell me about the dolphin."

That girl without makeup, the young, inquisitive child I imagined had once inhabited her body, appeared. Monica's eyes glistened, focused somewhere behind me on a fond memory. It was as if she had become a totally different woman.

"How did you know?"

"Know what?"

"That the dolphin is the one thing I contributed to the décor?"

"It felt out of place, so I knew it had to be a message."

"A message?"

"The universe calling to you. Have you always liked dolphins?"

She put her arms onto the edge of the tub, resting her head on them so she could make eye contact. She looked so different from the woman who had answered the door. She was almost incandescent, as if I had peeled away the edges of a thick cocoon to reveal a radiant interior.

"Right after the divorce and before Daddy got custody, Momma took me to Florida. We visited a dolphin research facility. Not a theme park where they perform, but a place where people study them. One of the grad students put me in a life preserver and let me play in this big holding tank where a half dozen dolphins were swimming. They all had injuries of some sort and were there to get well. Their resilience amazed my young mind. They seemed to know that someone had plucked them from the ocean to help them. They trusted these people they didn't know to fix them, with total faith that they would soon be free again."

"And you got to swim with them?"

"It wasn't at all like those places where you hold on to a fin and the poor things follow orders for food. It felt like we were friends, laughing and playing together. It was almost as if the play itself was part of the healing process."

I could picture it. And I was fascinated by Monica's total immersion in the memory. "I'm sure it was."

"Anyway, before we left, I was allowed to accompany a group that took one of the rehabilitated dolphins back to the ocean. I felt its elation when we set him free. He circled the boat, laughing and jumping. And then, he came back and touched my hand as I swirled an arm in the water, waving goodbye. It felt like it was saying, 'Thanks. I hope we meet again.'"

Monica's gaze had a faraway look.

"That was the happiest moment of my life. I keep the picture with me so I won't forget it."

I got onto my hands and knees so my nose could touch hers.

"I think I know what you were born to do, Monica."

"Work with dolphins? That's not in Daddy's plan."

"It is now. He just doesn't know it yet."

Monica's eyes were exploring my face. She was reassessing me.

"He'll take away all of this and the money."

"What do you care? You hate all of this, anyway. And you're twenty-eight, with your own resources. I bet you could talk Adrian into advocating for some financial aid for an advanced degree in oceanography or even veterinary medicine."

Her lips brushed against mine.

"Why are you doing this, David? What do you care about one fucked-up girl who has done nothing but treat you like shit since you walked in the door?"

"Here's what I see." I pulled back slightly so she could focus on me. "I see this amazing woman, spending every day of her life helping injured dolphins get well so they can enjoy the freedom that is every being's birthright. Yes, there will be danger, setbacks, and some shitty days. But if you are the person I think you are, you can redirect your powers toward your dreams. Stop sport-fucking to hurt Daddy and declare your freedom instead. Your life is too short and way too important not to spend it swimming with the dolphins."

Monica nodded. Her gaze seemed to focus beyond me as if she might just be visualizing the picture I was painting. Rapid eye movements told me she was processing a plan. As the bullet points fell into place, her anger evaporated. In its place was something new, exciting, energizing.

Monica touched my cheeks with the tips of her fingers, lightly pulling me toward her. The kiss she gave me was powerful in its tenderness. She didn't seek my tongue nor manhandle me like Adrian had. I imagined it might be how she would kiss a fish, the one thing she truly loved.

"I think I might be ready now," she said as I lifted her out of the tub and wrapped her in a giant beach towel.

"Ready for what?"

"Ready, at last, to be loved."

Monica rested a palm on my torso, slowly working southward as her fingers felt the hair on my chest.

I stopped her.

"Perhaps later, Monica. You have some work to do first."

I saw confusion in her eyes as I gently took hold of her hands.

"You are a beautiful soul, Monica. You deserve to be treated like a precious spirit. You will find the strength to make your dreams come true. It won't be easy, but you will make it so. You know your purpose. You know your joy. Don't wait another moment. Go for it now."

Her tears returned. But this time, I felt like they were tears of joy. She was envisioning her power, painting her own portrait of what she now knew she could become.

We walked to the windows. Monica contemplated the glow of the evening beyond the sheer privacy blinds.

"Telling me 'no' only makes me want you more," she murmured.

I turned her to face me. "Channel that desire in the direction of your dreams. Tonight, that's the best gift I can give you."

She thought for a moment. "The symbolism of what you won't do was just as important as what you did do. Thank you for that."

I planted a kiss on Monica's forehead. "Let your memories—good and bad—be part of past chapters. You'll want to revisit them from time to time, just to see how far you've come. Distance and life experience will probably allow you to interpret your story much differently."

"You're implying that I'll come to understand why my father did what he did."

"I think you already know. And perhaps you are beginning to see what you can do to help him."

"With the same acceptance and kindness you used to help me?"

"You will do it in your own way. It may not feel kind at the moment, but trust your gut, and your way will ultimately be the right way."

8

WHAT IS HAPPENING TO ME?

ELLEN

It had been fourteen days since Adrian and I had double-teamed David, and I still felt a delightful tingling sensation inside of me.

While his performance under the influence of my nutcracker recipe was beyond flawless, I would respect his wishes where alcohol was concerned.

And how I loved giving him permission to fuck Adrian's self-confidence back into her. They were so busy in that shower they didn't see me watching every move. Was it perversion or just a kink to get off by watching two people you care about getting it on?

All I could say was that they weren't the only two who were enjoying what they did that morning. David definitely had a gift. I intended to help him turn it into a career.

Since that day, he'd been over almost every evening after he finished work. One thing he must have picked up in his foster homes was how to care for babies. He took Elise off my hands when he came in the door. She already recognized his face and smiled when he talked to her. He was comfortable bathing her and changing diapers, and he jumped in to wash the dishes when it was feeding time after dinner. I still put her to bed most nights. David was adamant about respecting that activity as mother-daughter time. But sometimes, I'd let him rock her to sleep. I'd stand just outside the door, listening to him singing to her. His voice was so soft and the backstory so poignant that I couldn't help tearing up.

When she was finally down for the evening, our quality time began. The two of us stretched out at either end of the sectional, me with my wine and David with his Coke. We'd download the events of the day and talk about our hopes and dreams.

David told me about Elliot, the closest any foster father had been to an authentic dad, and the lessons he learned from a dozen nightmarish placements in lesser foster homes. He shared memories of his real parents and I came to understand how life had given him wisdom well beyond his years.

Here was what was odd. We never talked about this thing we had going on. It was as if we both were afraid of the implications and simply wanted to live in the moment.

As David predicted, our sex had grown beyond a solely physical thing, although we were still working out a lot of our painful pasts as we fucked each other's brains out.

The erotic moments I treasured most were when we lay side by side, connected in the most intimately physical way possible, just holding one another. We didn't have to speak. The warmth, comfort, and safety I felt were indescribable. Two hearts beating as one. Two souls in perfect harmony. It was the greatest peace I had ever known.

What was happening to me? I felt like I was in a blind high school crush. I couldn't get enough of David. How I wished there weren't such a vast age difference. I would have a ring on his finger in no-time.

I realized that David had never truly been in a relationship with a girl. His was a generation of fuck buddies and Facebook friendships. I wanted to help him experience as many women as possible, talking with him about what he learned from each afterward, like the older, more experienced female friend everyone wishes they had.

I texted my career idea to Adrian. She was on my wavelength.

She immediately responded, asking if she could "farm David out" to help a young intern at her shop who was struggling.

The very thought of talking with David about the whole thing excited me even more. In my selfish mind, I wanted him to become an expert in every dimension of the art of love: the physical, the psychological, and the spiritual. He would benefit; his "clients" would benefit. And, selfishly, I would be a beneficiary, too.

I guessed he had met the girl last night. That morning, he had texted me:

"Whew. Not at all what I expected. Can't wait to tell you all about it."

I couldn't wait to listen.

9

MEETING MR. HADEN

DAVID
　　Monica's newfound courage didn't take long to manifest.

I considered Adrian's generous internship offer and texted her I would take her up on it.

It felt a little surreal to be going to work in a suit and tie for the first time when I arrived at the office the next Monday to begin my adventure.

Adrian was waiting for me. "Whatever happened during your night with Monica Haden definitely altered her attitude. She quit cold an hour ago. No notice. Something about moving to Florida. Oh. And there seems to be another thousand dollars in your investment account."

I was happy for Monica. She was spreading her wings at last.

Adrian wiggled a finger and held up a pink phone-message sheet.

"The game may not yet be over. You have a command performance up the street."

The note said, "Mr. Haden expects David Orion at ten o'clock in his office."

I cringed. "Uh-oh. I hope this doesn't negatively reflect on you."

Adrian waved a hand as if she were swatting a mosquito. "Fuck him. I was looking for a job when I found this one."

"Mr. Haden and your CEO are best friends. I know snowballs like this roll downhill."

"Don't apologize before you know the extent of the shitstorm. Robert Haden isn't the only one in town with powerful friends. Just be yourself. Monica might need some air-cover, and you're just the guy who is fearless enough to provide it."

❧

RISING TO A CRYSTAL PYRAMID POINT AT THIRTY STORIES, THE Haden Building was the city skyline's defining structure. The Haden Corporation inhabited the top ten floors, with Robert Haden's private office at the very top.

An armed guard behind the granite welcome kiosk summoned two sumo-wrestler-sized security men to escort me into the elevator and up to the twin oak doors that were the executive suite entrance. That only heightened my unease.

Sumo Number One delivered a timid knock on the door. "Come in," a voice thundered. The pair opened the doors in unison, closing them behind me as I entered Robert Haden's inner sanctum.

The office was as big as Monica's apartment and then some. Haden's architect composed the ceiling of glass bricks that rose to the pinnacle of the building's pyramid elevation. The heads of wild game conquests hanging on the walls reminded me of a British hunting club's interior. A gargantuan conference table took up half of the space. An aerial view of the city framed Mr. Haden's enormous desk, a mahogany block, surrounded by a half dozen brown leather chairs. The king himself sat in a high-back throne, elbows on the polished desktop with hands clasped below his chin. He was squeezing his fingers so hard that they were red.

Haden unwound them just long enough to point to the center chair, already pulled close to the victim's side of the desk.

I sat.

"What did you do to my daughter?"

It was the opening I expected. I leaned across the desk, offering a hand.

"It's nice to meet you, Mr. Haden. I'm David Orion."

He ignored it.

"I know who you are. And I have a pretty good idea about what you did. I want to hear it from your own lips. What did you do to my daughter?"

"What did she tell you?"

"I'm used to being called 'sir' by underlings."

"I'm not your underling, Mr. Haden, and I'm not afraid of you. Do you want to tell me why I'm here?"

"She's gone. Monica left last night. She gave the condo keys to the servants. I know you were with her last week because she told me so. What happened?"

"We will not play the game this way, Mr. Haden. You tell me what she did, and I'll try to help you understand why."

The CEO's face flushed as his blood pressure rose. "We both know damn well what she did. She told me she was done with finance and wanted to play with fish. She told me I could keep my money if I didn't like it. And I don't. Now talk."

"She didn't like the life you mapped out for her, Mr. Haden. I think you know how she was rebelling against your micromanagement. All she did was tell me what she wanted from life. I told her she should talk with you about it—that a father who truly loved her would want her to be happy."

"What do you know about fathers?" Haden flipped open a folder on his desk. "David John Orion. Orphaned at age nine. Raised in a series of foster homes. An unimpressive student. Barely graduated from college. Got a job at Sandia Wealth Advisers by fucking the help."

I didn't like that last accusation, but I held my temper.

"Why are you such an unhappy man, Mr. Haden?"

The CEO's head shot back in surprise. His face reddened as his blood pressure rose. He mirrored the angry sneer Monica had given me that night.

"Nobody talks to me like that."

"I heard those very words from your daughter. Perhaps more candid conversations would be good for you."

Haden ignored me.

"I've already spoken with my lawyers. Two police officers are waiting outside of this office right now who will arrest you for prostitution, rape, and accessory to kidnapping the moment I press this red button on my desk. Know I can make those charges stick. You will end up in jail until you are too old to even think about a woman."

"Does it feel good to have people fear you, Mr. Haden? Were you bullied as a boy? Is bending people to your will the way you find fulfillment?"

Haden's hand hovered over the red button.

"Press it," I said. "I don't fear your threats. I have my own resources. They may not be as extensive as yours, but they are substantial enough to circulate the truth about how you were turning your daughter into an alcoholic and a sex addict. Yes, you have substantial holdings and considerable power. But you also have a board of directors and stockholders, some of whom will wonder why a man would tamper with judges to gain sole custody of his daughter so he could spend the next fifteen years emotionally abusing her."

Robert Haden crossed his arms in defiance. He leaned backward in the immense chair that was a perfect fit for the monumental desk as if there was an invisible force field between us. He was not used to being challenged by anyone. But I was on a roll and didn't give a shit.

"Let's not threaten one another, Mr. Haden. I would much rather help you regain your daughter's trust and affection. But that choice is yours. Are you able to focus the same courage and faith you applied to build this company that has your name on it to rebuild a meaningful relationship with the person in your life who is most important to you? Or is your addiction to power and position so deep that you would destroy her just to keep up the façade?"

The hand moved away from the button. Haden stood up, clenching his fists in fury.

"Nobody talks to me that way."

"Is that what you said to her? Just like that? How did that work out for you?"

He opened a desk drawer, producing a chrome-plated Smith & Wesson 357 magnum pistol. He placed the weapon on the desk.

"I may kill you myself. Everyone in this building will testify that it was self-defense."

I sat back in the leather chair, pulling my tie aside and ripping open the buttons on my shirt, exposing my chest. I should have been terrified. My life was just beginning, and it could easily end in the next few minutes.

But I felt strangely at peace. I could hear my mother's whispers. "Trust the universe, David. If your intentions are in the right place, things will work out." Ever since my parents' deaths, I had felt a conflict in my heart. I tried to do the right things. But there seemed to be a lot more sorrow and setbacks than were fair.

If life ended here, so be it.

"Do as you will, Mr. Haden," I said. My voice was rock steady. My gaze shifted from the barrel of the gun to his eyes.

I could see him processing things just as his daughter had before her breakthrough.

"Monica loves you desperately. She wants you to be proud of her. But you passed on to her the same hot blood that runs in your veins. She wants to do it her way, just like you did. Shouldn't you celebrate that? Shouldn't you encourage her to follow her heart? Killing me is easy. Show me you have the balls to answer my question. Why are you so unhappy?"

Robert Haden sank into his chair, his head tilting up toward the crystal spire.

"My father worked on the line for General Motors. Forty years. He sacrificed his own happiness, his health, and, ultimately, his life for us. He died just six months after he retired. Six months! He tried to convince me that this was job security, his version of 'The American Dream.' They broke him. I grew up watching him slowly wasting away. We argued about it. Oh, the fights we had. But I was determined to be in control of my fortune. I wasn't working for anybody but myself."

The CEO stood, pacing back and forth.

"It took years, but I studied the rules of business and the lives of the men who knew how to play the game. I learned their secrets and put them to work for me."

He circled the desk until he stood directly in front of me, holding out a pair of open, shaking palms.

"I built my company with these two hands, with determination, with sheer will. You could not imagine the sacrifices I made to create all of this. No child of mine was going to endure what I did. I would pass on everything I knew, and ultimately every dollar I earned so that my daughter wouldn't have to suffer."

The dolphin photograph I remembered from Monica's condo lay on its back in the frame I recognized from the condo. He picked it up.

"And this is how she repays me?"

He flung the picture against the wall. But the frame was plexiglass. It didn't break but fell to the wood-tiled floor, intact.

That gave me an idea. I pointed to the picture.

"You are living proof that a dream can't be broken. But a spirit can. You saw that happen to your father. Why would you do that to the most precious of your creations?"

Haden slumped into the chair next to mine, emotionally deflated.

"Her mother said as much when I divorced her."

"And what was our answer?"

Haden's voice was quiet. "I said that I knew best how to raise a child in my own image."

I leaned toward him.

"And you did your best. Sometimes our best isn't what the customer wants, and we have to reassess the product. I imagine that few men know that better than you do, Mr. Haden."

"Where does a twenty-three-year-old get the right to talk to me like that?" It was a halfhearted attack.

"One blessing of living in a series of foster homes. I saw a lot of different parenting styles, most of them profoundly ineffective. Like you, I became an old soul quickly and had to find my own way. The road to purpose still isn't clear to me. I know a lot of things that don't work, and I'm willing to risk everything to try something that might, even if it turns out to be wrong. That's the American dream, Mr. Haden. We each define it in our own way. Doesn't your daughter deserve the chance to write her own adventure story? Your dad sacrificed everything so you could have that chance. She's responding to you exactly as you responded to your own father. Shouldn't that make you proud?"

He made eye contact. "She hated that damned condominium. I built the thing just for her."

"Then take one percent of what it cost and invest it in that Florida dolphin tank. Endow the program at the university that trains the people who help heal these animals. You can give them every tool they need. But let them—let Monica—guide you. Give it lovingly, unconditionally. Even if she flames out and ends up doing something different, you will have contributed crucially to many lives. And your daughter will finally see how much you truly love her. Isn't that the legacy you really want?"

Robert Haden was lost in thought. It was suddenly as if I weren't there. I gently patted his shoulder as I stood.

"Monica is an extraordinary woman, Mr. Haden. Give her some wings and watch her fly."

"You're missing two buttons on your shirt. Not a very good impression on your first day in a new job."

Adrian was, as ever, acerbic and focused on the details. "Haden's doing?"

"I don't know, Adrian. Perhaps I'm learning that there will be some people I just can't help."

My friend leaned forward in the leather chair with the skyline view.

"It's an excellent lesson. Some you just have to let go."

"I feel bad for the old guy. He has a daughter who wants to make him proud. Now she knows how. I just hope that someday he can see the light."

Adrian put her thumb under my chin, turning my face toward hers.

"It's not your fault if he doesn't."

10

ONE YEAR TOGETHER

ELLEN
"I want you with me at all times," Ralph said, straightening his tie in the bathroom mirror. "You need someone to treat you like the royalty you are, and I'm just the man to do it."

He pressed a hand into his sport coat pocket, producing a women's diamond Rolex watch.

"For you, Ellen. A sign of good things to come."

Ralph flipped open his phone, pressing the calendar button.

"Now," he continued. "I have corporate events, Wednesday through Friday. You'll look good on my arm. I'll have my administrative assistant take over management of your calendar so we can stay on the same page."

I explored the contours of the watch with my thumb. Another controlling man. I sure knew how to pick em.

"Are there strings attached to this watch, Ralph? Or is it truly a gift?"

Ralph tilted his head as if I were speaking Chinese.

His response, when it came, was halting. "It's... a gift... No requirements... Just a dream. I see us as the new power couple in town. You will benefit from your association with my name."

I put the watch back into Ralph's palm and ran a finger down his right cheek. "No, Ralph. It's you who would benefit. I seek a partnership of equals, a relationship where we don't have to give up our individuality for the sake of the other person's insecurities."

I could see the wind deserting Ralph's sails. His arm candy was evaporating before his eyes.

"I could make all your dreams come true," he said. It was a half-hearted attempt. He had other prospects.

I leaned in to give him one last peck on the nose.

"I can make my own dreams come true," I said. "I wish you well with yours."

❦

TODAY MARKED THE ONE-YEAR ANNIVERSARY SINCE I HAD MET David Orion. We were going out for Italian tonight, and I couldn't wait.

He was doing great at Sandia, and he was on track to finish his MBA in the spring. His "other" profession took up most weeknights, but he reserved Wednesdays and weekends for Elise and me.

Kimberly was on my lunch card. She's one of the few high school girlfriends who had stuck with me through the juvenile drama, the marriage my parents hated, and the painful divorce. She was also unaffected by my suddenly outstanding financial position. She owned a successful business and had earned her own fortune. Money sometimes changed how people perceived you. My good fortune didn't change her at all.

Kimberly was one of the few people in my life who knew the entire story about David.

We had met at a hole-in-the-wall bar. It was classy enough that the drunks stayed out but also hip enough that it didn't really fill up until after dark. We had the place to ourselves.

"Damn, Ellen," Kimberly laughed when she saw me enter the place.

I wore tennis shorts and a sweatshirt. The jewelry was the only thing that gave a sense of my financial capacity. "I'm so glad you took that two-timing fucker to the cleaners. What does it feel like to be rich?"

"Well, I don't have to worry about where the next cable bill payment is coming from anymore."

Kimberly took a long drink of her wine. "No shit. And you've moved up in the world. Remember how we used to make fun of the bitches who live in your current neighborhood?"

"Who would have thought we would both become them?"

Kimberly was dancing around the questions she wanted to ask, as a good friend sometimes did. So, I helped her out.

"I know what you really want to hear about."

"David!" She nearly swooned. "What's it like to have a virile, young lover at your beck and call."

"He's definitely virile and young, but he's not at my beck and call. The age difference is a big deal, and we both respect one another's independence. He's supportive of my exploring other men, and I am trying to help prepare him to be the best husband a woman could wish for."

Kimberly's face darkened. "That asshole ex-husband always talked down to you. He was the law school rock star, and you were the retail major he pulled out of a dead-end job to be his wife."

"It wasn't a dead-end job. It was the dues you pay to earn the job you really want. Brad was just a cute guy with a silver tongue. I knew the week after I married him that something was wrong."

"Like banging that other woman?"

I winced. Brad's infidelity still hurt. "I didn't realize it then, but he was doing it pretty much from day one. But the idiot didn't sign a prenup. You would think a lawyer would be smarter than that."

"He knew how to play the market. Your half of his pile is darn amazing."

"I'm still comprehending that one, Kim. But I'm grateful that I got enough to make sure Elise can have a stay-at-home mom."

Kimberly's eyes got misty. "So tell me about David. What's he like?"

I sighed. Just the thought of him aroused me. "Imagine the best sexual experience we ever had in high school or college. Multiply it times ten. You'll get the idea."

"But he makes his living fucking other people. Isn't that what your ex was doing?"

"He's not my husband, Kimberly. I encouraged it. I want him to know as many women as possible so he can parse the wheat from the chaff. Somewhere along the line, he'll meet the right one, and I will have prepared him well to be a god to her. And, of course, I also get the 'benefits' of what he learns from the others."

"And what about you? The age difference feels like a lot now, but in another decade, it will be—what's that word we learned in French class? De rigueur?"

"No. We are both trying to find true soulmates for one another. I set David up with clients, and he has encouraged me to date."

"And how is that going?"

"Oh, I have probably been with a half-dozen men since I met David. The problem is that the older they get, the more baggage they bring to the party. The best men my age have partners."

"What does Elise think about all of this?"

"Jesus, Kim, she loves David. She never really knew her real dad. David speaks to her on her level. It's fascinating to watch him talk to her as if she's a grownup. She's smitten, too. David drops everything to help me care for her when she's sick. He's the one father figure she's ever known."

"In the bedroom, Ellen. What's he like to fuck?"

"Think about every erogenous zone on your body, Kim. He knows mine with map-like precision. He's figured out the nuance of how I like to be loved and delivers it. Only it's a little different every time, so I never know when or where he is going to pull the ripcord and take me for the ride of my life."

Kimberly shuddered. "Jesus, just hearing that is making me wet. Why are you willing to prostitute this rare gem with other women?"

"He's not a prostitute. God, that word totally doesn't fit David. He gets inside a woman's head. He won't even take you on unless he thinks he can help empower you to grow and find your happiness."

"Well, two failed marriages since high school make me one hell of a candidate for improvement. But I wouldn't want to impose on a good friend."

That was exactly what Kimberly wanted to do.

I wrote David's cell number on a napkin. "Try him and tell me what you think. I've been working with him long enough that he knows just about every move and when to make it. If you're like other friends I've pointed toward his erection, you'll be dying for more. Just bring a big wallet. I don't want him to feel he has to do this his whole life, and I'm teaching him how to build a nest egg."

"If he's so good, why don't you marry him?"

That was the question I was avoiding.

At first, I thought the relationship with David would be a brief adventure. But the more we got to know one another, the more comfortable we were. I was younger than my years and in my sexual prime. David was an old soul, patient, generous, and caring, with what felt like no strings attached. The more men I dated, the more I appreciated my freedom from commitment and friendship with this phenomenal human being. That his body aroused me in an instant was very sweet icing on the cake.

But I guessed I still thought this would be a temporary thing. Young men move on. I may have money, but I didn't have a purpose beyond Elise and riding him until we both passed out from exhaustion.

"The age difference is a thing, Kim. I don't want him to have to push me around the old folks' home when he's still got life in him."

My friend answered me with the wisdom I didn't have. "I think the age thing is meaningless. Nobody can predict the future, Ellen. If you've found your soulmate in every other way, to hell with political correctness. Marry the boy and fuck one another as long as you still have the backs to do it."

I laughed it off. But deep inside of my heart, the desire for what I thought was a more normal family continued to eat at me.

"Our relationship is still dawning," I said. "There will be plenty of time for both of us to grow. And damn it, I sure have a lot of growing to do."

When we finished our salads and Kimberly stumbled to her car, she turned back to hug me.

"I have to ask you this, honey. How would you really feel about my contacting him?"

"You're in his sweet spot, Kim: the right age, no husband. The kinks I know you have are already on his menu. Take a taste and give me a full report."

"I have never, ever had a girlfriend give me permission to fuck her boyfriend before. You two really do have a unique relationship."

"We are both learning about life and one another," I said. "And in reality, we are probably two very horny ships, just passing in the night."

❧

I THOUGHT ABOUT THE LIFE MY PARENTS HAD TRIED TO FORCE ON me and the traditional housewife life Brad had in mind. There was a very clear picture of my perfect partner. David's face came into focus when I thought about many of the dimensions of the ideal. None of my other conquests were even close.

A year is no time at all. Keep looking. Like David says, "We ultimately find what we seek."

⚜ 11 ⚜

KIMBERLY

DAVID
"The voicemail says she's a high school friend of yours."

It was our regular Wednesday evening together. Elise was in bed, and we were in our usual repose in the family room.

"Kimberly! You will love her. She owns Chakra's Day Spa and is a licensed masseuse. The place is five-star. And so is she."

"Anything I need to know about her?"

"She's tall."

"That's it?"

"Oh, there's much more. But I'll leave that for you two to discover. Please her."

With that cryptic tidbit, I responded to Kimberly's invitation. Her instructions were explicit. "Nine o'clock on Thursday at the spa. Come prepared for some exercise."

I ate a light meal Wednesday evening and headed for the football weight room. Since Kimberly was a special friend of Ellen's, I wanted to make the best possible first impression.

By nine, Chakra's Day Spa was closed for the night. The cleaning people had done their work. The employees were long gone. The owner was the only one who remained.

When Ellen said that Kimberly was tall, that meant six-foot-three, an inch taller I was. She self-identified as "big-boned." She wasn't fat but could have likely been a good halfback if her high school coach would have allowed her to go out for football.

She also knew all the tricks to carve what God gave her into a genuine work of art. Masculine muscles blended perfectly with feminine charms. Like Ellen, she was a blonde, but her hair was thicker, braided into a ponytail that danced behind her as she gave me the VIP tour.

The circuit ended at one of the massage rooms, lit only by scented candles. Kimberly prepared the table with heated flannel sheets. A variety of lotions and oils filled a shelf above a cedar-lined dresser like an apothecary.

She leaned against the dresser, taking another visual pass over my short-sleeved, casual collared shirt, cargo pants, and flip-flops.

"Do you dress like this around the house?" she asked.

I couldn't control the laughter. It was the right question.

"No, ma'am. This is work attire."

"Ellen and I have been BFFs for ages. Throughout everything, I've never been envious of anything she had, until now."

"My uniform does that to you?"

"What's under it does that to me. Knowing just a little of your love story does that to me. That you will attend to my needs when you have such a precious gem waiting for you at home makes me wet."

"There is no reason to be envious, Kimberly. Tonight, I belong to you. How can I please you?"

"Oh, God." She exhaled it, arching her back. Her nipples pressed against the fabric of a thin linen shirt. She'd left the top buttons undone to show me something of what lay behind the light material.

"Let me begin by doing something for you. I'll give you the massage of your life; only this will be developmental. As I work on you, I'll teach you what to do and where to do it, to bring your women to climaxes that they will remember for the rest of their lives. Then we'll switch places, and you'll practice on me." Kimberly quivered as she said the words. "Until you get it just right."

It was another of those surreal moments where I still couldn't believe this was happening to someone who was climbing telephone poles and running from barking dogs a year and a half earlier.

Kimberly took a step toward the door. "I'll wait outside for a moment so you can get comfortable on the table."

I blocked her exit, standing close enough that she could smell the body wash from my shower at the gym. "I've got a better idea. Why don't you undress me? And perhaps you would feel more comfortable without that top on."

I unbuttoned it. One by one, the small circles that held the shirt together released. The figure revealed was magnificent.

Kimberly returned the favor. I was less than an hour out from my time in the weight room, so every sinew retained its definition.

Her gaze feasted on my pecs and the six-pack abs I worked so diligently to chisel. I had purposely left my boxers in my gym bag. When she unbuttoned my cargo pants, they fell away, unveiling what I knew was her favorite part of the male anatomy.

She couldn't take her eyes off of it.

"Lie face down on the table. I'll cover you with some warm blankets."

"It's okay to skip the openers," I said, "and jump ahead to the part where you put your hands on me."

Kimberly was determined to do this right. Her first few touches were lasting, lingering, and determined. Practiced digits examined the contours of my body and explored my hair. Her thumbs kneaded and rolled recalcitrant muscles into submission. Gentle fingers swirled across my temples in a slow, circular movement that calmed me down and fueled my desire at the same time. She steadied her palms just above my chest hair, floating up and down my torso until she found every erogenous zone, including several I didn't know existed.

I was both surprised and pleased with her mindful approach to her craft. As she worked with my various muscle groups, she described how to find and release tension and how the heat generated by friction could produce pain or pleasure, depending on how and where you applied it. And she gave me a new-age lesson in chakras, the seven primary energy centers balance to create harmony between mind, body, and spirit.

She flipped me over at half-time, putting a warm washcloth over my eyes and forehead as she kneaded the muscles in my neck where I have always carried my stress.

"And now, about the G-spot. You'll be practicing this in a bit, but I'll give you a sense for how to find it."

Kimberly hopped on top of me, straddling my hips with her long, lithe legs.

"Insert a finger with your palm facing away from me. Curl that finger like you're trying to stroke my belly button from the inside. It has a little more texture than the surrounding areas. You'll know it when you feel it."

I followed the instructions. Kimberly was right. There was a slight roughness I could sense on the tips of my fingers. I stroked her on the inside with one hand, working on her pearl with the other.

Her eyes rolled toward the ceiling. Her sensual moan was deep and guttural, a lioness teaching her king how to please her. I pretended not to notice.

"How about the other erogenous zones? What are your favorites?"

"Oh," Kimberly gasped, pulling herself back into the moment. "Everyone has places on their body that turn up the heat. I love it when you run your tongue between my tits. Anywhere on my neck is a slice of sexual heaven."

As Kimberly instructed me, she was working her way down my hips, legs, and feet.

The room smelled of rosemary and lilacs. The oil glistened.

"How do you decide whether to use lotion or oil on a customer?"

"Most people prefer lotion because it's easier to wash off. I'm using oil because it will be much more fun fucking each other when we are both slippery."

Kimberly enjoyed the response she saw as my procreation instinct starting to kick in.

I was relaxed, renewed, and ready for her. "I love the fact that when we stand, I can look directly into your eyes. When I first saw you, I knew that we were both going to enjoy this very much."

There was a difference in the tone of her voice. It was less academic and more sensual. "Being tall and tough scares men away. Having someone who appreciates me as I am is marvelous."

"My desire for you goes well beyond your spectacular body, Kimberly. Your accomplishments as a businesswoman, your incredible dedication to your art, and the way you have channeled your knowledge into fashioning that incredible body—it all makes me want to know so much more about you beyond the alluring sexuality driving me wild."

Kimberly's cheeks reddened. "Do you talk to Ellen this way?"

I grinned. "All the time."

"She's crazy. I would never let you out of my sight."

"Ellen says that these little adventures benefit everyone involved. Who am I to argue?"

Kimberly rinsed her hands in a small sink near the table. When she turned, it was a single button that released her slacks. As they fell to the floor, I could see the crotch area was saturated.

"I don't know if Ellen told you, but she and I share something in common."

I didn't have to wait long to find out.

"There was one time in college where we both blew two guys at the same time. You can imagine that scene."

She giggled when she saw how her words made my blood flow toward her ultimate target.

"Take me back to that moment," I said. "Right now."

Kimberly's tongue circled the point where my balls pressed my scrotal sack outward. It was another instance when I was grateful for the skills of an experienced woman.

I lifted my head from the table to see her entranced by the thickening pole that was rising in concert with my heartbeat each time her tongue touched me.

There was anticipation in her voice. "Young meat. It's been such a long time."

"Are you objectifying me?"

She nodded, sliding an expert tongue up and down my shaft. "Oh yeah."

I didn't stifle the groan. "You'll hear no objections from me."

I was fully erect now. Kimberly coaxed me to a ninety-degree angle with her ring and little finger, tasting my production with the tip of her tongue. It took every bit of my practiced self-control not to explode right then.

It impressed her. "*Oh*. You're good. I've never known a man who could get past that move without shooting his wad. I guess I'll have to work a little harder."

I was balancing on my elbows now. Kimberly watched my abs flex as I sat upright, putting an oily hand behind her neck and pulling her toward me.

"A small gift of gratitude for one of the best massages I've ever had."

She would have opened her mouth to receive me, but I held it shut with my thumb as I teased her warm lips with my own.

"It's the nuances that transform fucking into something a little more personal," I whispered.

I allowed her jaw to relax as our tongues began their explorations. While girls my age seemed to be more prone to demolish me, Kimberly, like Ellen, was much more sensitive. I learned to respond in kind, and the effect was powerful.

I felt a slight bobbing as I kissed her. Kimberly was doing some explorations of her own nether regions.

I gently pulled her away from her work to find Kimberly's fingers glistening.

I drew back slightly so she could focus. I licked each finger in turn. Then I returned my attention to her mouth so that we could both savor the flavor as I ushered her hand back to the source of its wetness.

"You taste wonderful," I said as our tongues continued their mating dance. "Let me practice my G-Spot skills."

Kimberly didn't need any additional incentive. She swung a leg over me, kneeling on the edges of the table, lowering her mound to my waiting mouth.

I began at the bottom of her labia, licking upward toward her clit, tickling its base, and then sucking it with increasing pressure. I knew precisely how Ellen liked it done, inserting my two middle fingers inside Kimberly and beginning the back-and-forth motion that Ellen called "David's wave."

I found the spot Kimberly had described.

Reading her face like a speedometer, I carefully increased my tempo and suction. It took Kimberly to orgasm. As her muscles clutched my fingers in a vice, I knew what lay ahead of me as our sex progressed.

"You aren't following the plan!" Kimberly tried to make it sound like she was angry, but I knew it thrilled her. She dismounted and moved toward her original aim. "This was what was supposed to be next."

She encircled the head of my shaft with those fantastic lips and sucked as she wrapped both of her fists around me. She slid her hands gently upward with each pull of her mouth as if she hoped to draw my contributions at her command. Kimberly was enjoying every aspect of the task. I didn't want to disappoint her.

I allowed my hips to thrust upward as if she were lifting me off of the table.

And I thought of Ellen. It was her face I saw as I made love to Kimberly. Assigning her spirit to her best friend gave me all the power I needed.

The warm white liquid flowed. Kimberly pressed her hands against my body and drove down on me. She sucked down cascade after cascade.

She licked her lips as I finished. "Imagine Ellen and me doing this to two guys at the same time."

I grinned. "I would have kicked my competition to the curb. Two against one is my favorite scenario."

With our twin passions temporarily under control, we switched places. Kimberly was again the teacher, guiding me through every move she made during my massage.

I added some choreography when I rolled her onto her back, flicking the tips of her nipples, attending her lips, eyelids, forehead, and cheeks. She turned her head, presenting an earlobe. My tongue examined every detail. I ended up dancing back and forth across her ripening pearl. When I was confident that it again aroused her, I stood back from the table, admiring my work.

"Do I have a future?"

"Oh, yes!" She groaned the words, swinging upright and off the table. She took my hand, pointing toward the sauna. "Let's go turn up the heat."

Describing the act of sex may seem repetitive, and the actual activities involved are, in many ways, identical.

What we remember are little things that make each interaction special. Kimberly appreciated a partner who could keep up with her vast reserves of sexual energy. And I enjoyed the raw power of her physicality. In the privacy of her establishment, nobody cared how loud she screamed or how the walls of the place felt like they might crumble under the relentless collision of my body against hers and then hers against mine.

Some of her approach was downright virile and masculine. Her orgasmic clutches gripped me like a vice. I worried that I might lose my condom.

But by now, I knew what to do to please a woman on her terms. I trained for this marathon and did not stop until I satiated Kimberly.

I could also tell when there was something there that shouldn't be. But that conversation could wait.

When we stumbled into the shower together, our muscles felt like rubber, every bit of sexual energy spent.

She was thoughtful, putting Coca-Cola in my wineglass, and toasting our experience with her preferred vintage cabernet. Clad in warm bathrobes, we sat in a pair of overstuffed chairs. The sounds of a synthetic waterfall that covered a far wall mixed with soft music, permeating our consciousness in surround-sound stereo.

"Are you happy?" I asked.

"Totally. An old soul in a youthful body. The perfect combination. I warned Ellen that if she didn't marry you, I would."

I knew that part of her history. "Why didn't marriage work for you, Kimberly?"

She shook her head in resignation. "Number one was a high-school sweetheart. We were too young and too different. Number two wanted babies. I desperately love kids, but there are too many children out there without parents and I wanted to adopt. That opened a can of worms that revealed other fundamentals that didn't fit. Giving it up was mutual."

I ran a finger around her beautiful lips, realizing how moved I was by this.

"One of the few benefits of bouncing from foster home to foster home is how you get a sixth sense for someone who would make a great parent. Anyone you brought into your life would be so lucky to have you as a mother."

"I sometimes wonder about that. I have a ton of flaws. You've seen just one dimension of who I am."

"Here's what I've seen. I've witnessed the teacher patiently guiding her student toward excellence. I've witnessed the tender Kimberly, who understands that each person she meets has a heart that may have been broken along the way. And I've definitely witnessed the exuberant Kimberly, who attacks life with an infectious passion. Yes, it's just the tip of what may be a very complicated iceberg. But you have all the fundamentals that would make you a wonderful parent."

"Now, if I could find a man who shared my vision. I'm sure Ellen has told you how tough it is out there, especially when you are playing the game in your thirties. We are still wrestling with acquiring wealth, and self-image is about growing a career. It's almost impossible to tell if a person has soulmate potential."

A small flame of inspiration shone a light on an old memory. "I'm not sure that's the case. I might know someone who is exactly the man you are seeking. But before we talk about your future, there's something I want you to check out in the present."

I sat on the arm of her chair. "May I take one more liberty?"

She looked confused but nodded.

I took her hand, sliding it inside of her bathrobe and gently palpated her left breast, where my explorations had made the discovery.

"Can you feel it?"

Her face turned ashen. "Yes."

"First thing tomorrow morning, I want you to visit your doc and get a mammogram. It may be nothing, but please don't take any chances."

I could see her processing the information, moving through the emotional spectrum from stunned silence to fear.

"I'll tell you what," I said. "You'll sleep a little better with someone by your side who cares about you. I think that perhaps this might be a good night for me to get to know your bedroom."

Kimberly tried to put on a brave face. "I'll be okay. You don't need to do that."

"I know you'll be okay. And if you don't want company, I respect that. But I also know what it's like to get bad news when you're alone. We've become intimate friends tonight. And holding you when you're afraid is what intimate friends do. Just know it's out there if you want it."

She decided she wanted it.

12

DATE NIGHT IN POST-OP

DAVID
As I feared, the mammogram had revealed a lump. It was large enough to require surgery.

I learned then that I shared something else in common with Kimberly: We both had no immediate relatives.

Ellen and I were her family that day. We sat in the waiting room as the procedure took place.

It took two-and-a-half hours. We couldn't read anything on the surgeon's face when he finally appeared.

"She came through procedure fine. She struggled a bit with the anesthesia, so there may be a few uncomfortable post-op days ahead. The good news is that we got it all, and what we did won't significantly affect her breast's physical attributes. We also took two lymph nodes. Everything is on its way to pathology."

He crossed his fingers. "Now, we wait."

It devastated Ellen. Had I felt anything similar in my explorations with her? No, nothing. She was determined to get her own mammogram early. "Just to be sure."

Ellen was anxious as I walked her to the front door of her home.

"What can we do to ease Kim's fears while we wait for the results?"

I had already been pondering an idea. Ellen's emotional reaction when I explained my plan confirmed it was a winner.

❧

KIMBERLY HAD A ROUGH TIME RECOVERING FROM THE ANESTHESIA. She was in and out of consciousness for the next forty-eight hours. By the evening of the third day, the nurses told us she would be lucid enough for visitors.

I knew that they would bring her an evening meal at seven.

At 6:45, I stopped at the nurse's station for directions to Kimberly's room.

When the night duty staff saw me, jaws dropped.

I stood before them in a black-tie and a tuxedo, complete with patent leather shoes and a boutonnière. In one hand, I held a small vase with a single red rose in it. My kit for the evening was in a bag I held in the other.

"Can you ladies direct me to Kimberly's room, please?"

One nurse finally came to her senses and led me in that direction. "Are you family?" she asked.

I nodded, a little white lie, but one I intended to play out.

"She doesn't have anyone on the list. I'm really not supposed to give out any information."

"I promise you that whatever information you tell me will remain between your patient and me. After all," I pointed to my outfit, "who but a significant other would do this?"

The nurse nodded, holding up a small piece of paper. "She was too out of it when the doctor came today. This is her pathology. I was going to give her the news when she wakes up."

I managed a wink. "Okay if I do it? I'm with her, no matter what the doctor says."

The nurse gave me the folded diagnosis that I was still too afraid to read.

When I entered, Kimberly was asleep, her hospital bed tilting her into an upright position, a nasal oxygen cannula wrapped around her neck.

It gave me time to prepare. I set the rose on the adjustable table where they put her meals, placing a wine glass on either side. I quietly uncorked her favorite cabernet, setting it next to my ever-present Coke can.

I pulled up the special playlist on my phone's music application, connecting a small wireless speaker to the device. Whatever the news, I was prepared to help her face it.

Then I waited, leaning against the far wall. I wanted the full scene to be the first thing she saw when she woke up.

Kimberly stirred. Time and oxygen had helped clear the persistent aftermath of the anesthesia from her body. The eyes that opened were tired but clear.

She had trouble processing what they were telling her.

"Good evening, beautiful," I said. "I promised you another date. I decided I couldn't wait until you were ambulatory."

In my peripheral vision, I saw the entire night crew was standing in the doorway, watching us.

Kimberly kept shaking her head. I could imagine the mixture of fear, elation, and surprise that must have been going through it.

I poured us each a drink.

"You're supposed to be pushing liquids, my dear. May I serve you?"

"David." Her voice was still hoarse. "What did they find?"

"Let's drink first. 'To living life to the fullest, one day at a time.'"

She tentatively took the glass I offered, and we clinked them together. She barely managed a sip.

I frowned. "That just won't do. All of it, please."

She complied.

"How long have I been out?"

"Two days. Long enough for us to have some important information to share."

I felt myself grasping for control of my own emotions. Sparked by the visceral memory of my personal losses, tears streamed down my face.

Kimberly steeled herself. I watched her back straighten as she put her glass on the table.

"Tell me."

"The good news, my beautiful warrior, is that they got everything. Your boobs are going to remain the superlative works of mother nature's art that they always were."

"And?"

I took out the white piece of paper the nurse gave me. Holding my breath, I scanned it.

The wave of relief was immediate and immense. "The tumor was benign. They took two lymph nodes just to make sure. No cancer, Kimberly. Now get over this damn reaction to your drugs, and let's get out of here."

Whatever shields we fought to maintain crumbled. Tears flowed. I slid in next to her in the tiny hospital bed and held her close, feeling the choking inhalations between Kimberly's sobs. I cried, too. I cried for Elliot's wife, for my mother and father, for Mr. Haden and his daughter. And for this brave soul who was beginning her second life tonight.

There was more.

I pressed play on my cellphone. Johnny Rivers sang "Slow Dancing (Swaying to the Music)." I lifted her from the bed and onto unsteady feet.

"May I have this dance? Just put your arms around my neck. I'll do all the work."

"The fuck you will," she said. The news was sinking in, and her strength seemed to rush back.

With Kimberly's head resting on my shoulder, we circled our small dance floor as the Johnny Rivers tune became her all-time favorite song.

I saw the night shift crowd still standing in the doorway, not a dry eye in the bunch.

"When you're up to it," I whispered into her ear, "the next after-hours session at Chakra's is on me."

Kimberly lifted her head from my shoulder, kissing me with surprising vigor.

"And after that," I added, "there's someone I want you to meet."

13

ELLEN'S TURNING POINT

DAVID

Kimberly was on the mend. The Haden adventure was quickly receding into memory. And that kernel of an idea I'd had after our night of passion blossomed into a plan.

"Elliot!"

"David? David Orion? Am I really talking with you?" The man on the other end of the line still recognized my voice.

The foster father who had convinced me to go to college let go of one of his trademark laughs. It always began deep in his belly and bubbled up into explosive mirth.

"Kilauea," we called it, after the volcano landmark he knew well from growing up in Hawaii.

"You should have called me when you graduated. I would have come to your commencement."

"I wanted to, my friend. But I wasn't sure if it would dig up memories that you might still be processing."

"Anita." He said the word as if it were a prayer. "Yup. I still have some bad days, and I miss her like crazy. Cancer is a bitch, David. You were with us for one 'normal' year before it hit and had to watch her die in my arms. That couldn't have been easy for someone who lost his parents like you did."

"How are things?" I asked. The question was purposely vague. I wanted to allow him to share what he felt comfortable sharing.

"I'm on the mend, David. She would want it that way. But man, running a foster home with five kids and no wife is wearing me out!"

"That's why I called, Elliot. Do you think you might be up for a date?"

❦

I WAS EXERCISING MY LEFT BRAIN IN THE WORLD OF FINANCE, TOO, fully immersed in my internship.

Adrian assigned me to Sandia's top securities analyst, a hot stock picker named Thomas Stafford. Tom didn't cut me any slack. We shared every assignment they gave him, each of us doing research and comparing notes. I found I had a gift for analytics. In short order, our teacher-student relationship strengthened into a friendly competition, sometimes heatedly debating the merits and risks of an investment.

Things seemed to go well with Adrian and Lance. I added another prohibition to my personal checklist: never have sex with a co-worker. Adrian accepted this, although I knew that I would be tested if her current relationship cratered.

Ellen gave me the space I needed to chase my degree and build the foundations of a financial career. Although we both encouraged one another to date others, we still enjoyed those regular "magic moments" she promised, both coming away from every encounter with a deeper connection.

I was well into the second year of my internship when I saw her name on my caller ID toward the end of the workday. I knew something was wrong the moment I heard her say my name.

We sat across from each other in the enormous family room I knew so well. Ellen had been crying.

"Brad called me from LA. He's getting married again. And she's pregnant."

We both knew that her ex-husband was the wrong partner for her, but hearing this news must have triggered Ellen's unworthiness gene.

"I know, I know," Ellen said. "He's a total asshole, and not being with him was exactly the right thing to do." Her face crumpled into a sob. "But how could he choose her over me?"

By now, I had developed a sense of when to give Ellen her space. She didn't need a lover now. She needed a listener.

"I realize that I have all of this money, but I still don't have a purpose. This news just reinforces how empty I feel inside."

"Elise is two years old, Ellen. And you can hire a nanny if you wanted to pursue a career."

"But what, David? What would I do? How could I possibly add any value to anybody?"

Ellen saw me tilt my head, fact-checking what she had just said.

"Add value to anybody besides you, my love. I need a larger purpose to feel worthwhile. I think about that every day."

We needed a date night, stat. "Text your mom. We'll drop Elise off at your parents' place and go someplace quiet, where we can brainstorm over dinner."

Ellen glanced at her reflection in the window glass. "Oh, Jesus. I'm a hot mess. Can you call her while I get ready?"

I wasn't sure that Ellen's mother totally understood this thing that her daughter and I shared. She seemed satisfied telling her friends I was Ellen's "protégé" and welcomed my attention as a grandmother might appreciate an attentive grandson. When I told her I was "surprising" Ellen with a last-minute dinner, she quickly agreed to hang with Elise.

I found my two girls in Ellen's bathroom as she was putting her face back together. She held up a bottle of foundation, clearly unsatisfied with it. "What do I have to do to find makeup that works for me? This is crap."

Elise giggled. She was just beginning to mimic simple words. She grinned at me.

"Crap, David. Crap. Crap. Crap."

Elise waddled around the edges of the huge bathmat next to

Ellen's rain forest shower, singing, "Crap. Crap. Crap. La. La. La. Crap. Crap. Crap."

"That's your child," I said.

Ellen frowned in mock disgust.

I swept Elise up into my arms. "Let's watch Mommy get pretty."

"Between my allergies and my coloring, I can't find any makeup that makes me look the way I want to look."

"You look just fine with nothing on," I said. When Elise again seemed about to parrot something embarrassing, I added, "With nothing on your pretty face."

"Pretty face, Momma," Elise said, reaching to touch Ellen's cheek. "Pretty face, Momma. Me too, please. Me too, please."

I flipped the child around so I could nuzzle her nose. "You are perfect, just as you are, Elise. Beauty is in the values of the beholder."

"Isn't the phrase, 'eyes of the beholder?'" Ellen asked.

"A sociology prof enlightened me on that one, sunshine," I answered. "Every society has its definition of pretty. Women among the tribes of Africa would laugh at the war paint you girls wear. And think about how some kids my age like cosmetics that help them maintain an image that implies no makeup at all. What we value drives our attractions."

Ellen squeezed one of my pectoral muscles, shaking her head to try to clear out a salacious thought. She focused closely on the round, fun-house mirror that amplified her eyelashes as she painted them with mascara.

"All I know is that everything I've tried is sh—" She saw Elise in her peripheral vision. "—schlock."

Ellen sighed, intently focused on her preparation. "If I had a million dollars, I'd start my own damn company."

Another idea germinated in my mind. But that could wait for dinner.

WE SELECTED MARIANO'S FOR THE MEAL. WE BOTH LOVED Italian food, and Mariano's had the combination of excellent cuisine and a quiet atmosphere where friends could become lovers over linguini and sangria.

Ellen sipped a glass of the fruity stuff. I added lime to my Coca-Cola for the occasion.

I leaned on a palm, admiring her by the electric candlelight. "You are a beautiful woman."

"Says one of the few who have seen me without make-up," she said, attacking her chicken piccata.

"If you could tell one of the cosmetic companies to make you what you wanted, what would it be?"

Ellen focused on her entrée, pontificating as she slurped away. We were both technically adults, but we weren't above talking with our mouths full if Elise wasn't around.

"It would be hypoallergenic so people with sensitive skin could use it, and I would have a zillion shades so people of every complexion could find a match. And I would have a fragrance line, too. There's been nothing interesting invented in that space in ages."

She noticed me giving her my rapt attention, my head resting on both of my palms.

"What?" she said. "What are you looking at?" She pulled back, giving me an artificial frown. "You realize, David, we are in a public place."

"I don't see anyone but you. Keep talking."

She went back to devouring her meal. "I'm just saying, if I had a million dollars, I could do better than what's out there now."

"Listen to what you just said, Ellen."

She paused, a long string of pasta hanging from the side of her mouth.

"What?"

"That's it. That's the thing. You have a million dollars. You have a zillion dollars. Why not go out and start that company?"

Ellen waved away the idea. "What do I know about business?"

"You know how to surround yourself with smart people who can fill in the blanks. That's what you told me the day we met. You're the visionary, the brand, the face of the company. Hire the worker bees to turn your vision into a reality."

"You're so wonderful, David. But I don't think you understand all the moving parts in a business like that."

I took her fork from her hand, twisting a long string of pasta around it and feeding it to her.

"This is a fork. This is the pasta. This is your mouth. We didn't make the fork or the linguini. But we know what our taste buds like, and we are paying somebody in that kitchen to give us exactly what we want. What's the difference?"

I pulled a pen from my suit coat's pocket and started drawing on a napkin, holding the finished product up for her inspection. It was a poorly rendered cursive logo.

Corbin Cosmetics.

⚜

WE LEFT MARIANO'S WITH FULL STOMACHS AND VISIONS OF A cosmetics empire dancing in our heads. Elise was already sleeping when we picked her up at Ellen's parents' place. After tucking her daughter in for the night, Ellen rolled her eyes and held her hands over her stomach.

"Oof. I'm going to need an extra hour in the gym tomorrow to work this one off."

I backed her against the wall and planted one of the more sensual kisses she taught me onto her lips.

"I can think of another way we can burn some calories."

"David! My breath is all garlic. How could you even be interested after the meal we just ate?"

"Let's find out!"

I turned around, motioning for her to imitate Elise and hop onto me for a piggyback into the bathroom. This act of childish fun made her giggle. So did the limerick that I was glad Elise wasn't awake to hear.

"Ellen's the woman for me. She makes love like a wild chimpanzee. The smell of her breath may scare others to death, but for me, it's as sweet as can be.

"Chimpanzee?" She swatted the top of my head from her perch. "So what does that make you, King Kong?"

I growled in my best gorilla voice. "Let me put you down, and I'll show you what the Empire State Building looks like with all the lights on."

Ellen grinned. "In some ways, David, I hope you never grow up."

We were now very much like a married couple. Spontaneity required preparation. We stood side by side, undressed, and focused on flossing, brushing teeth, and washing our faces. As we completed our ablutions, our eyes met, and we shared a common moment of enlightenment. Even impulsiveness had a routine. It seemed so silly. And we started laughing.

We couldn't stop ourselves.

Ellen's mirth grew. It began with shoulders that shrugged when she tried to suppress it. She closed her eyes and held her breath before giving it up and melting into a puddle of laughter.

"I was just about to complain that it was time for another bikini wax," she said.

I frowned. "Come to think of it, I've never had one. How do you think I would look with a Brazilian?" My nose started to run from my convulsions.

Everything we said made us laugh harder. I threw Ellen over my shoulder and carried her to the bed, dumping her onto the center of the mattress and jumping beside her.

"Are you full, ma'am, or would you like some dessert?"

"To hell with the Empire State Building. Show me your cannoli," Ellen said.

"Only if I get to taste your Tiramisu first."

Ellen propped her beautiful torso on her elbows. The view did its work on my libido.

"I have just one thing to say to that," she said, finishing the sentence with a tremendous belch. "Now waste no more time. Take me! Take me now before this pasta moves through my system and I have to take a dump."

Ahh, the language of love.

We were well beyond the dating stage, where the filters evaporated and we said exactly what we meant.

I rolled on top of her, being careful not to put any weight on her belly.

"As you wish, Princess Buttercup."

Ellen cackled as I slid down toward the Tiramisu and worked on the frosting. But instead of responding sensually, she reacted as if I were tickling her ribs. Ellen writhed, laughing harder and harder with every movement of my tongue until she finally pleaded for me to stop.

I flopped down next to her. In time the laughter subsided, and we could catch our breath.

"I guess I taught you something tonight, after all, my love," Ellen said. "Sometimes, sex is fucking hilarious!"

We both burst into another round of laughter, falling into one another's arms and, soon after that, drifting into a deep, satisfying sleep.

As I watched her eyes close, I whispered into her ear.

"I, the great ape Kong, can foretell your future, my dear."

"And what is that," Ellen answered dreamily.

"Corbin Cosmetics. It's going to become a reality."

❦ 14 ❦

SATURDAY

E LLEN
By now, I knew David, the lover, well. I was learning about David, the man.

At its best, sex should be a tool for empowerment and affirmation, not a weapon for selfishness and personal pleasure. Its many dimensions could enrich or harm a relationship. The physical act was just the tip of the iceberg of love. Affirming self-worth was the goal of David's work with the increasing number of women who are better for being his "clients." He hoped to illuminate the light of personal power that already shines within them, to free their minds from past pain, and to chase the bright future that is out there for all of us, if we can just open our eyes to it.

I felt like the greatest beneficiary of David's gifts. I was proud to have been able to play a minor role in helping him discover his own definition of happiness . . . and to chase it.

I managed a clandestine lunch with Elliot, David's last foster father. The burley Hawaiian had definitely been a positive influence. I could sense David's thoughtful side in his gaze as we sipped iced tea and attacked our salads.

"You're filling many roles for David," he said. "For better or worse, we all fall for women who remind us of our mothers. But be aware. David's selflessness is also a weakness. He's used to sacrificing everything for everyone else. Standing up for what he needs isn't part of his mindset. I hope you'll develop a sense for those moments and call him out. He deserves to receive the same love and affection he manifests so easily."

I blushed, suddenly uncomfortable. "I hope I'm doing the right things, Elliot. I want David to be happy."

Elliot smiled. The laugh I heard David describe rumbled up from his broad chest. "Oh, he is. Don't let the paradigms you both carry blind you to what's really going on. What you two share is special. I'd hate to see either of you get hurt."

I could never imagine hurting David. Elliot's admonition felt over the top. I wrote it off to a dad looking out for his favorite son.

৩৯

KIMBERLY ASKED ME WHAT I LOVED BEST ABOUT OUR relationship. I came up with the following list:

David prioritizes the team. The only time I see him anywhere near angry is when he feels that Elise is getting short shrift. He loves it when the three of us do things together.

"When you help someone win, you win."

He has said that so often that Elise is parroting it when I tuck her in at night. A valuable lesson learned early.

He remembers the small things. He leaves little notes on my bathroom mirror when he is up and out while I'm still sleeping, always affirming and always appreciated. I get flowers for no reason. And some nights, my mom will show up to watch the kid because David had an impetuous date night idea and couldn't wait to do it.

He and Elise make me breakfast in bed on Saturday mornings. It usually ends up with having to wash the sheets because it became a family affair and the crumbs get everywhere. We watch kid shows on my bedroom TV and have tickle fests that leave us all exhausted from laughing.

He made us a "coupon book" filled with fun things we can do

together. Some include Elise, like a trip to the zoo or a date night with ice cream. But others are all about the two of us. I still love reading proper books, so he'll take me to my favorite rare bookstore and turn me loose. We split up when we walk in the door and rejoin two hours later. One time, I went looking for him and found him in an overstuffed chair, deeply engrossed in one of C. S. Lewis's *Chronicles of Narnia*. His mother read it to him when he was Elise's age. I could see a tear at the base of an eye. David slowly shook his head.

"When all is said and done," he murmured, "the memories remain." It was one of the rare times when I could truly see the pain he had lived, growing up with nothing like a traditional family.

And he loved to read to my daughter. Some of my warmest memories of our time together will be the golden hour before her bedtime, with the three of us sitting on the couch, Elise ensconced between us as he worked his way through her favorite book series. Some people just read. David performed, making the tales come alive. Elise always wanted one more chapter when it was time for bed.

He's always prioritized bedtime as mother-daughter time, but I secretly knew how much he loved rocking her to sleep. When I heard them giggling and whispering, I sometimes snuck into the doorway to watch him massage the bridge of her nose with his index finger. Even before she could talk, he did that to help lull her to sleep.

He whispered the last line from his favorite song to her as she drifted into dreamland.

"Goodnight, Chipmunk. No matter what you do, I will still love you."

Then, we retreated to the living room to pick up the land mines of toys and books. I poured myself a Malbec and prepared David's Coca-Cola. If the weather were warm, we sat together on the porch swing and watched the stars.

David pointed out the constellation that bears his last name and said, "Whatever happens and wherever you are, I will always watch over you."

We wrestled with complicated conversations about parenting and purpose, about our hopes and dreams, about life. But we still avoided talking about a future we might have together.

David had always maintained his own apartment. Even though we spent eighty percent of our time with one another, this nod to independence still felt essential to both of us.

On the nights that I couldn't convince him to stay with me, we held each other in the doorway.

"You are the best thing that has ever happened to me," he said before gently pulling away. "No matter what you do, I will still love you."

I couldn't count the number of times I'd dragged him back into my bedroom after hearing that line.

To fall asleep with his hand resting on that corner where my hips and my ribcage meet. To wake up in the middle of the night and move that hand upward, surrounding a breast and gently squeezing it. To feel him thickening against my ass even as he continued to sleep. The regularity of his breathing and the humidity of his exhalations tickling the hairs on the back of my neck. And his natural aroma—that thing some people define as pheromones—if I allowed myself to drink it all in, I was on top of his perfect body in an instant, feeling his pulsations inside of me, begging him to squeeze my tits as I slid my clit back and forth over the sensual roughness of his pubic hair. By then, he was awake and totally focused on my pleasure. But not in the selfish way Adam and Ralph took me. I could see the love and respect in his eyes. His movements mirrored my own, as if he were totally dedicated to helping me achieve happiness in every possible way.

I'd lived long enough to know how rare this was. Yes, David was young. But for me, he was the standard against which I judged every other man. With him, I felt empowered, safe, respected, supported . . . loved. Finding that combination in a person nearer my age had been impossible so far.

"Dammit, Ellen, you're in love," Adrian would say. "You have the perfect man right before your eyes, and you refuse to let yourself see."

But I didn't see it. I wondered, was this Elliot's message, too?

There was an unspoken agreement that David and I would enjoy the moment. But we both assumed that moment would eventually pass.

It feels as if life were a series of seasons. Some were stormy, some had sunshine. Each could help us grow if we are open to the lessons that each season brought.

Whoever David ultimately chose as a life partner would be the luckiest woman in the world.

And I prayed that there was someone out there for me who shared the qualities I so admired in this amazing young man, a gift from the universe who always strengthened and renewed me, who honored the strong woman I was becoming, and who would love me in good times and in bad.

When my David years concluded, I would feel an immense hole in my heart. But I would try to fill it with gratitude for the gifts we had given one another in this transformative chapter of our lives.

15

SWIMMING WITH THE DOLPHINS

DAVID
Ellen spun up one hell of a New Year's Eve party. Her house was full of scientists, marketers, lawyers, bankers, and her array of treasured friends. Clutches of LEDs adorned the trees. Caterers were at every elbow with food and drink. It was a little too cold to be outside, but the steam that rose from the pool added a paranormal vibe to the festivities.

In the six months since our Italian date night, the notion of Corbin Cosmetics quickly had grown from two words on paper into a full-fledged C-Corporation. A phalanx of attorneys and money people drew up the architecture of the new venture. Ellen had found her purpose. She became absorbed in making her dream real.

Our trysts became less frequent. But that was okay with me. Between my studies, the internship, and a referral client base that seemed unending, life exhausted me.

The sheer volume of requests reminded me that the world had too many under-appreciated souls in desperate need of affection and affirmation. I felt content to help ease their unhappiness.

Adrian had set my rates, demanding that my service fees be much higher than I dreamed possible. I still inhabited my small apartment and augmented Ellen's generous seed money in my investment account with a ton of cash.

We were in one another's arms at midnight, kissing and toasting a new year that neither of us could have ever envisioned. A growing cadre of friends and colleagues who admired her and invested in her now surrounded Ellen. Many had become Corbin Cosmetics employees. Elise was in seventh heaven, being allowed to stay up late. All seemed well with the world.

ELLEN

A LIST OF THE THINGS I WAS GRATEFUL FOR:
Good health.
Good friends.
My beautiful daughter.
The purpose of a new and exciting career adventure.
David.

WHEN I WOKE UP ON NEW YEAR'S DAY, HE WASN'T IN BED NEXT to me. I could hear laughter in the kitchen. I tiptoed to the doorway.

David and Elise were making pancakes. She had the spatula in her hand, and David was guiding her as she flipped them on the griddle. Pancakes were everywhere: on the counter, on the floor, one even stuck to the edge of the vent fan.

"You are getting better with every flip, chipmunk!"

"Let's flip another one, Uncle D. I want to surprise Mommy with breakfast in bed."

"That's a great idea! Let's do it!"

"Someday, I want you to bring me breakfast in bed."

David consulted his watch.

"How about today! When we finish cooking, you can run back

and jump under the covers and pretend you're sleeping. I'll bring you some pancakes and orange juice and wake you up with a kiss on the forehead, just like I do for your mom."

"You don't kiss her on the forehead, Uncle D. I watch you."

"Really? How would you describe the way I kiss your mommy?"

"Like you love her. I'm happy that you and Mommy love one another."

"I am, too, chipmunk. Ready to flip some more pancakes?"

That got to me. I had never been happier than I was right now. David was a huge part of that happiness.

I still hoped that we would both find our special someone.

But when that happened, I knew a part of me would die inside.

۞

DAVID

I arrived at my cubicle at Sandia Wealth Advisers on the first day of business after the holiday and found a plain white envelope on my desk. It had my name on it and the words "Haden Corporation" in the upper left corner.

The message inside said only:

International Airport – Executive Terminal – 2 p.m. Today.

When I showed it to Adrian, she shrugged. "Either he's taking you on a world tour or flying you to a desolate corner of the desert to have you killed."

I cocked my head. "Do I have life insurance?"

Adrian looked at me like I was from another planet. "Of course, you do. Elliot is your beneficiary. I wouldn't tell him, though. Your favorite foster father might get ideas."

Aside from the two pilots, I was the only soul on the Cessna Citation.

"Anyone want to tell me where we are headed?" I asked as the co-pilot pulled the handle to secure the exit door.

"SGJ," was his answer, the three-character designator for St. Augustine Airport in Florida. "There are refreshments in the refrigerator near the restroom. We should be there in a little less than three hours."

Nobody told me I couldn't use my cell phone, so I popped open the GPS application and watched the aircraft wending its way southeast. In time, the blue-gray water of the Atlantic Ocean appeared on our left. As the plane touched down and reversed thrusters on the runway, I could see the words "Northeast Florida Regional Airport" painted on the main terminal building.

I recognized the man at the wheel of the long black limousine that took me farther south on State Road A1A. It was one of the sumo-sized security guards from my visit to the Haden Corporation. Thirty minutes later, we turned into the parking lot of the Florida Aquatic Mammal Research Center.

The sumo opened the door, and I saw her.

Monica Haden.

Her skin reflected the sun's golden caress. Gone were her implants. What remained was still stunningly alluring. Her blond hair had morphed back into its natural mahogany brown. Her body was slender, graceful, and strong. A pair of cutoff jeans and a bikini top were partially covered by an oversized blue T-shirt with the Research Center's logo on the front.

But it was the aura surrounding her that showed me Monica's dream had finally come true.

"David!"

She jumped into my arms, wrapping her flip-flop-clad feet around my waist and covering my face with kisses.

"Come see what we've been able to do."

Construction vehicles were hard at work behind a sign that said, "The Future Home of the Haden Aquatic Veterinary Medicine Institute." Monica hugged me again as she inspected the activity. A new hurricane-safe brick structure grew out of the ground, topped by a broad solar panel array. Huge saltwater pools tagged each end of the facility. Its architecture had a Frank Lloyd Wright flavor, mixing form and function in a way that spoke of elegance and power.

Monica glowed. "Daddy did this."

It wasn't the hard voice of the unhappy woman I had first met. It was more like the playful laugh of a young girl on Christmas morning.

"Come meet everyone."

We walked up a flight of stairs and through a doorway. Spread out before me was another vast circular saltwater pool. The water's dance reflected the sun like a bowl of turbulent diamonds. A group of dolphins raced in circles, swimming just inches from the ceramic tile flashing.

"Is this the place?" I asked. "The place where you first met your friends?"

Monica shook her head, the broad smile still on her face. "This is the place. But the pool is brand new, much bigger, with state-of-the-art equipment."

Several other people were there, examining the half-dozen dolphins bounding through the water.

"Everybody," Monica called out, "this is David. He's the real reason I'm here."

I was surrounded by a group of twenty and thirty-somethings, who looked like they had walked out of a Jacques Cousteau documentary. Bearded men and lithe women in shorts and swimsuits held medical instruments, carried clipboards, and punched numbers into data pads.

There were no handshakes here. Instead, we exchanged powerful hugs as if we were old friends.

"Monica is a godsend," one woman said. "She seems to have a way with these animals. We study them, but she is one of them."

The man with the clipboard added, "When the Institute is finished, we will be one of the top three dolphin research facilities in the world. Our study on dolphin communication and intelligence is already circulating as a Ted Talk." He put his hand on Monica's shoulder. "This one did the talking."

"You guys are the magicians," Monica said, deflecting the praise. "I still have a lot to learn."

She wrapped an arm around the man's waist. He tickled the top of her head with his clipboard. "David, meet Dr. Frank Holland. This lab is his baby."

"Monica has told us so much about you," Frank said, "but nothing about what you do, besides conjuring up miracles like a magician."

Monica winked at me. "David is an 'interpersonal relations consultant,' an expert at how to maximize human performance. One of those wonderful people who doesn't get enough of the spotlight but works real magic behind the curtain."

At that moment, I knew what I would print on my business cards.

Frank shook my hand the way I did, one in the grasp and another over the top. "We can't thank you enough, David. Because of your help, we'll be able to move a step closer to our ultimate goal."

"What's that?" I asked.

"To change the world, of course!"

Monica turned to me. "So, David, want to meet my friends?"

I thought I just had. I was wrong.

One man tossed me a bathing suit. Not waiting for me to change, Monica peeled off her T-shirt and dove into the pool. The dolphins immediately circled around her.

A moment later, I joined her, feeling accepting, shiny nuzzles and squeals as her friends checked me out.

Monica pointed to a dolphin missing its tail. "We're crafting a prosthetic fin for Jeremy here. Jere had a run-in with a great white. In another month, we'll have him back in the ocean, test driving our latest invention."

Monica introduced me to each fish in turn, telling their stories as if every dolphin were a family member at a reunion.

Monica was radiant. This was what success looked like. Ellen had introduced me to my gifts. Adrian was my test pilot. Kimberly was client number one, a friendly one who just needed a little self-confidence. Monica's metamorphosis and the trials that came with it clarified my purpose. For the first time, I felt a sense of what that purpose might be.

"Almost feeding time, Monica," Frank called from the pool deck.

"For us, too," Monica whispered to me. She nibbled on my ear. "I don't know about you, but I'm ravenous!"

She took me to a small cottage, walking distance from the Institute. A few pieces of functional furniture sat atop a hooked rug. Pictures of Monica and her dolphins filled oak-paneled walls. She fired up the small stove that was part of the living room, dining area, and kitchen. Compared to her father's condo, these were Spartan accommodations. But it was all Monica.

"I paid for every penny of this out of my earnings," she said. "Dad's job is to concentrate on the construction project and to help me with the foundation."

She could tell I was still very much in the dark as she flipped a pair of grouper fillets into a frying pan.

"We direct The Haden Foundation for Aquatic Research. Daddy is the treasurer."

"Who is the chair?" I asked, already guessing the answer.

Monica grinned. "I am. Being Daddy's boss has been a trip."

We dined on fresh fish, kale salad, and oranges. I was happy to note that Monica was drinking guava juice. There was no sign of alcohol in the cottage, not even a bottle of wine.

"Way to go, sunshine," I said as we finished our meal. "I knew you could do it."

Monica beamed.

I was still having trouble processing Mr. Haden's one hundred and eighty degree turn around. "How is your relationship with your father?"

"Once he understood that, in my own way, I was following in his footsteps, everything changed."

She ran a hand across my shoulder and down my arm.

"He's really a very affectionate man. Another trait we never knew we shared in common."

I asked the question that had been bothering me since I had boarded the jet. "How does he feel about my being down here?"

"It was his idea."

We washed the dinner dishes together as Monica talked about her plans for the future. She was entering the veterinary medicine program at the University of Florida, at last, a course of study that was totally her idea.

When the last of the silverware rested in its drawer, Monica took my hand. "Let me show you the rest of the place."

The rest of the place turned out to be a small bedroom, a queen-sized bed encompassing most of its square footage. Monica pointed to a photograph of the Florida night sky that hung on the wall at the foot of the bed.

She snuggled up to me on the edge of the mattress. Her natural scent was intoxicating. "Can you see it?"

Above the ocean, the Orion constellation stood guard, his belt and sword pointing toward the waves.

"You protect me every night, David."

It was a stunning work of art.

"Where did you find it?"

"It was a present," she waited a moment so her next words would have an impact, "from my father."

Monica rose and stood in front of me. She untied the neck and back strings that held her bikini top in place, letting it fall to the floor, revealing two perfectly proportioned, unaugmented breasts. Her rich, brown areolae and the white skin outlined by her bronze suntan rose and fell sensually with each breath.

I stood, removing my T-shirt. My arms encircled her waist. I felt the warmth of her skin against my chest.

Monica Haden looked deep into my eyes. I could feel her own telepathic powers at work, projecting strength, healing, and joy.

"Thank you, David. Thank you for validating my dream, for showing me what love felt like, for telling me 'no' when I needed to hear it, and for risking your life to back me up."

"How did you hear about that last part?"

"Daddy told me everything. I'm not the only Haden whose life you saved."

The look of desire that I knew well was evident on Monica's face. She put her arms around my neck.

"I haven't made love to anyone since before we met. Sport

fucking and booze are the old me. I plan to choose who gets to know me intimately with much greater care."

Our mouths found one another. Monica's kiss was tender yet probing and confident. My passion was rising. Tonight, she was more than just a client. The psychological distance that gave me the ability to be a witness without getting caught up in the drama was gone. We were two devoted friends about to share the most intimate of connections. I turned up the intensity, consuming her with a hunger that I usually reserved for Ellen.

Monica ran her tongue around the edge of my earlobe. "You told my father I had to do things my way. Let me love you my way tonight."

She guided me to lie on my back on her bed, eyes closed, arms and legs slightly spread.

"Dolphins can feel the presence of life in the currents that surround them," she whispered. "The slightest sensation can speak volumes."

Her gentle kisses and a warm, sensitive tongue began their ministrations.

Monica worked her way down from my forehead to my shoulders, across my chest, and up and down each arm. I was never sure where the next touch might be; the suspense mixed with sensation was powerful.

"It's all about the chakras. Every fiber of your body is interconnected, just as every living being shares a psychic connection."

I felt overwhelmed. This was Monica transformed—brilliant, purposeful, and happy. It was a dream I envied, growing up in a world where fear overpowered faith, wishing for happiness I couldn't even define. Each of us had made our dreams come true. My physical manifestation was so engorged as to be almost painful.

When Monica's tongue dabbed its tip, the sensation was nearly more than my well-honed self-control could endure.

"For humans, there is no greater intimacy than the moment where two spirits become one."

She applied a condom with delicate precision. A moment later, I was inside her.

It took every ounce of my willpower not to come. My eyes remained closed. My body was now so sensitive that I could physically feel Monica's aura before she rubbed my nipples against her own. I could sense her breath in the instant before her lips brushed against mine.

"I always dreamed that this was the way one should have sex with someone they care about," she whispered, "a compassionate, thrilling exercise in discovery, the ultimate expression of honor and respect."

Her tongue parted my lips, and my mouth opened to receive hers. Her exploration was both gentle and exuberant at the same time. The motion of her body felt like warm waves washing over me, her strong inner muscles pulling me deeper into her tidal pool with every sequence.

I read about the practice of mindfulness in school. In a way, it was already hard-wired into my being, a competitive advantage that others called "attention to detail." This was the first time I understood the role it could play in heightening both the significance and the physical pleasure of sex. That a woman with so much pent-up anger found the capacity to understand the true meaning of passion with such clarity was a miraculous irony.

As we made love, time stood still. I couldn't tell you how long we did it. But I'll never forget its culmination.

It began with the slightest increase in her tempo.

"It's all right to open your eyes now, David," she said.

What I saw was a self-assured, caring countenance, gratitude personified, totally focused on guiding our mutual satisfaction to its ultimate conclusion.

"Shall we share the moment together?" she whispered.

I nodded. There seemed to be no need for words.

"Let it go, David. I'm ready."

I thought I was the expert on self-control. But the minute she felt me stiffen, her own orgasm began.

The synchronization that Monica and I shared was total, the summit of mutual stimulation. I was thankful we were both mindful of birth control because it felt, at that moment, like every element was in place for conception.

We became two statues, completely aware of every minute sensation going on inside that place the poets describe as "The Portal to Ecstasy."

As the world again resolved into focus, we lay in one another's arms, talking until dawn. Monica recounted her heated conversation with her father, how she had disobeyed his command, taking just a few belongings, cashing out a secret bank account where she had slowly built a small savings, and boarding the plane for Florida.

As usual, business kept him from acting immediately, giving Monica time to confirm that her feelings about her career desires had increased in the years since she had first swum with the dolphins. She quickly connected with the team at the tank, beginning as a volunteer before her special connection with the animals became clear.

When Robert Haden had tracked her down, he had witnessed the sheer elation she felt in her new role. In the interval, his altercation with me had given him a lot to think about. It hadn't taken long before he understood that his daughter was expressing his same drive and desire in her own unique language.

Things happened quickly. Monica had an emotional reunion with this changed man, which conjured a warm past memory of a father holding a new baby in his arms. Robert and Monica Haden had recognized that they had lost one another once. They didn't want to lose one another again.

I knew that Monica had at last found her wings. My work was done. She drove me back to St. Augustine, talking nonstop about her plans for the foundation, medical studies, and a life living and working with fellow travelers who shared her passion, with her own father now her biggest cheerleader.

When we kissed on the tarmac as I was about to enter the Citation, we knew it might be the last time. The mindful state she had taken me to the night before was still with me. I could feel the energy flowing between us in our final embrace.

"What about Ellen?" Monica's question came out of the blue. "I think she's the one and only you were born to be with."

The one and only. I liked the sound of that.

"It may take time, even a little heartbreak before you realize it, David. But when you do, don't waste another moment living without being committed to one another."

I shook my head. "How did you get so smart?"

Monica grinned. "I had a really good teacher."

When I boarded the plane, she darted back up the stairs and handed me a thick, padded envelope with a note in her handwriting. "Open when you get out of the limo."

I was grateful for the three hours of solitude at 35,000 feet. There was much to ponder. I had found a meaningful and profitable niche. It was a profession with no actual competition, where I got to choose my clients and enjoyed rewards that were both financial and intrinsic.

Perhaps, I thought as the Citation turned on final approach, both Monica and I had truly discovered our purpose.

Sumo number two was waiting at the executive terminal, ushering me into the limo at the foot of the aircraft stairs. I sank into the thick leather backseat and closed my eyes, trying to be mindful of the sounds of the highway and the automobile. But now that I was home again, it was Ellen's face I saw. I was eager to tell her about my adventures.

"We're here, sir."

It was the first time I had heard either of the sumos speak. I stepped out of the limousine, surprised to see the towering Haden Condominiums in front of me.

"Miss Haden reminds you to open your envelope," he said.

I did. There was a note and a key fob inside.

Dearest David,

On behalf of my father and myself, please accept this small token of our appreciation. You know I always hated that fucking condo. I'll never, ever live there again. As Daddy and I tried to think of how to begin to repay you for the profound impact you've had on both of us, it seemed like providing a comfortable home base was appropriate.

Daddy's lawyers have executed all the paperwork.

The place is yours, David. Free and clear, with an annuity that will pay for maintenance and fees for the rest of your life.

Please rip out anything that doesn't reflect the amazing man you are and make it your own.

With deepest gratitude and admiration,
Monica and Robert Haden.

16

DAMON

ELLEN

   "If you want to crack the UK market, it helps to have a 'fixer.'"

Wade Simon's voice had the royal accent down perfectly. Any hints of his Scottish birth had vanished by the time he had graduated from prep school.

"I have the perfect man," Wade said as we shared an Earl Grey and scones at the Ritz in Piccadilly. "Member of the House of Lords. Involved with two successful start-ups here and one in the States."

"Hire to your weaknesses," was my motto. When we decided to branch out to Great Britain, Wade was the first person I had called. I was beyond trying to fake it when I didn't know something. "What does a fixer do?"

"We need a man with contacts at the highest levels of government, a man who knows the Richard Bransons of the world, a man who can easily fit in at any gathering from day laborers at the pub to Windsor Castle."

I was interested. "Who is this man of the world? And why don't I know his name?"

"Because we haven't met yet."

The baritone came with the perfect elocution I expected. Its owner was about my height. He had the physical build of a runner, dishwater-blond hair, a perfect set of teeth I knew had to have cost a fortune, and a Saville Row wardrobe that would have made Ian Fleming jealous.

"Damon Winslow at your service," he said. "Wade tells me I might add a little value to your enterprise."

"Ellen Corbin," Wade said, rising to his feet. "Meet your knight: Sir Damon Winslow, CBE."

I caught my breath. Damon's smile revealed some delightful dimples. His eyes had a calm confidence in them. I could see something else in them, too. He was enjoying the view.

"I'm told you can smooth the bumps and help us launch Corbin Cosmetics in Europe."

"I have been privileged to be involved with the GBTel introduction and consulted with Richard when he was considering a similar venture to yours."

Wade nodded as I sought confirmation. The Richard was Richard Branson.

"And why didn't Richard expand into cosmetics?"

"It didn't fit his brand image. He understands the business and could well be a future investor. Your gender and the viral nature of the demand for your products here should be more than enough to get us all the support we need."

Damon Winslow was still standing. I motioned him to sit with us. Wade raised a hand to alert our waitress. In moments she was back with a Vesper Martini in hand. I looked at my watch. Tea time didn't feel like a place for a martini.

"One of my many faults," Damon said, noting my inspection. "Gave up smoking last year. Made a vast difference in stamina for my running, and..." Damon tipped his head slightly forward. "And other things."

"I think you two should have dinner tonight, without my encumbrance," Wade said. "Perhaps you would consider Le Gavroche, Ms. Corbin? I've taken the liberty of making a reservation."

Michael and Albert Roux founded Le Gavroche in 1967. Some of the world's greatest chefs had emerged from their tutelage. Albert's son now ran the place. Another bucket list item ready to be checked.

"That would be delightful," I said, looking to Damon for confirmation.

Another bow. "It would be an honor."

⚜

"BE CAREFUL. HE'S A LADY KILLER."

That was the text Adrian sent back when I told her I was headed to dinner with Damon. I knew little about him but trusted Wade's judgment and was eager to learn how he could help us.

Our dinner together ended up covering more than just business. Damon was a charming, engaged partner. By ten that night, he had coaxed my life story out of me, texted a half dozen friends and colleagues to get balls in motion for our launch, and spoiled me rotten with the most expensive French wines and winning recommendations from one of London's most expensive menus.

Damon put me totally at ease. His personal magnetism was indisputable. Everyone, even mildly accomplished, seemed to know him. He made sure that all who came to our table to stroke his ego knew about me, our company, and our plans.

"The Fragrance that Facebook brought to England" was his impromptu tag line. It was true. When a British celebrity decided that Corbin Cosmetics were must-have items, she took to social media to opine how hard it was to "get what she wanted" at home.

The not so subtle sexual reference did the trick. We were shipping two million dollars' worth of product to the islands every month. It made sense to secure a manufacturing foothold in Britain.

I felt strong, secure, and ready for anything. What a difference a year makes. From poverty to prosperity to the CEO of my own company in eighteen months. Not bad!

Damon's hand grasped my own as we emerged on Brook Street. "Let's head to Charing Cross, and I'll show you some sights."

His ability to mingle with our fellow underground travelers on the Bakerloo Line and his deep connections with government and business opened doors. Security at Westminster treated us like royalty. Even with Big Ben under renovation, Damon somehow got us inside the guts of the famous clock. We stared through the scaffolding, taking in the slowly rotating London Eye and the ever-present boat traffic on the Thames.

"I'll wager that I convince you to become an ex-pat within the year," Damon said, snaking an arm around my waist. "Now, let me show you the best accommodations in town."

We were soon entering a suite on the fifty-fourth floor of The Shard, the tallest skyscraper in the European Union. The Shangri-La Hotel occupies eighteen floors of the South London landmark. I could feel the Zen-like tranquility that travel critics rave about amidst the Asian styling in the spacious lobby.

"My London retreat," Damon sighed. "When you work as hard as we do, it's important to recharge in a place where you know the service will be five-star."

I sat on the edge of the bed, drinking in one of the best views in the city. Damon slid next to me. Another Vesper martini, shaken, not stirred as James Bond liked it, materialized in his hand.

"Married?" I asked.

We were working our way toward utilizing that bed.

"Never," Damon answered. "Many girlfriends, but none who wanted to go the distance."

"One husband in the rear-view mirror," I said. "I actually owe all this to him. If he hadn't been such a scumbag, we might still be hitched. Mr. Right has eluded me so far."

"What about the kid?"

Was he talking about Elise? Or... "David?"

"I hear they call him The Lover Whisperer and you taught him everything he knows."

I blushed. "It's been a two-way street and I'll always honor him for that. But we both agree that we should find someone who is closer in age and a better fit."

Better fit definitely sounded like it came with sexual undertones as I said it. The wine from dinner was still doing its work. Damon was looking pretty damn good.

He rested his chin on my left shoulder. I could feel the warmth of his breath and smell the scent of his aftershave as he whispered into my ear,

"Sometimes, that person can appear when you least expect it."

"You?" I tried to sound incredulous. I liked the notion.

"One step at a time, m' lady," Damon cooed. "I find you intoxicating. Let's take our time and trust the universe."

He began with a gentle kiss on the neck. I wondered who had briefed him on my erogenous zones. This guy wasn't a loser. Perhaps he was the equal I sought?

"Girlfriend?" I asked. It was a weak attempt.

"No commitments at the moment," he said. "I'm feeling one coming on."

His eyes shifted to my chest. I took his hands in mine and selected one of the twins for his palpation.

"Show me how an Englishman pleases his lover," I said.

Our mouths met, and we fell backward onto the mattress.

17

MANDY

DAVID
My unique profession continued to prosper. One encounter always led to another, and I soon found myself with more clients than time. Besides the many one-night stands, there were some regulars. Patricia was a wealthy divorcee who owned a hotel chain and met me every Tuesday so I could watch her drink before our gymnastics. There was Linda, whose husband asked me to care for her sexual needs so he didn't have to; Meg, the cop, sought me out on the recommendation of her psychiatrist, and Dorothy paid me just so she could watch me shower.

I tightened the rules of engagement. No cheaters, no BDSM, and no insatiable twenty-year-old college students. We had to meet first for coffee to check one another out and agree on the assignment. That was sometimes tricky because I might run into another client at the coffee shop. That wasn't a problem unless they knew the woman I was vetting. In most cases, the previous patron would pat her friend on the shoulder and whisper, "Have fun. You'll love it."

The women I saw usually had a high net worth. Most came from one or more failed marriages, bodies sculpted to perfection by the plastic surgeon who could not cut out the low self-esteem that remained on the inside, and a flexible schedule that allowed for absences without questions.

Perhaps that was what made Mandy so interesting. She was none of the above.

⊙⊰⊙

I WAS EXCHANGING TEXT MESSAGES ACROSS THE ATLANTIC WITH Ellen about the merits of various pre-schools for four-year-old Elise when Mandy approached.

"Mr. Orion?"

I stood and held her chair for her. "Please. We're already friends. It's David."

What looked at me across the table was a wary, perhaps even frightened woman. Mandy's brown hair was straight, shoulder-length, and unkempt. A layer of insulation that was evidence of an atrophied life softened her curves. The green eyes behind her glasses had stories to tell. Her vibe gave me the sense that she was afraid to tell them.

I intertwined my fingertips, leaning my head on top of them, projecting the interest and admiration I truly felt.

"Mandy. I'm so glad to meet you."

She averted her eyes. "Monica Haden told me I should call."

Monica and I still corresponded regularly; in the Facebook era, it felt like we were neighbors.

"That's fantastic! Monica is a treasured friend. How do you know her?"

"College," Mandy said.

I wondered if we would get past these brief sentences.

"I'm honored, Mandy. Are you interested in some coffee or something cold to drink?"

She shook her head.

"Talk to me about life," I said. It was my conversation starter to negotiate the whys and whats of our transaction.

"Aren't I supposed to be telling you what I want when we . . . you know."

"There's no hurry, Mandy. Let's get to know one another. If you want me to go first, I'll tell you a little about me. I'm twenty-four and have been an interpersonal relations consultant for three years. I also am a financial analyst. Not married. I've discovered that I like to travel. I was an orphan and lived in a ton of foster homes. And I worked as a cable repairman before inventing this job."

"I work in mergers and acquisitions for a multi-national company. It's still a man's world there, and I chase the pipe dreams nobody expects to come true. I'm thirty-eight. Never married." She opened her palms, shrugging with embarrassment as she gestured toward herself. "Who would want this?"

"We can work on that mindset, Mandy. How would you like me to please you?"

She squinted her eyes as if just saying the words were painful. Her voice fell to a hoarse whisper.

"I like to give oral sex."

"Just *give*? Or do you like to receive it, too?"

"Give."

"Okay. Sounds good. We have our date and time. Tonight at eight at your place. We're actually neighbors. Haden Condominiums seems to attract the best and brightest."

Mandy ignored my compliment. "I'm good with money. I want to live someplace pretty, even if I'm not. And since I don't have a boyfriend or many friends for that matter, I have little to spend it on."

"You have a friend now. I'm very much looking forward to being with you tonight, Mandy. Do you want me to wear anything special?"

She thought for a moment. "A bathrobe."

"You got it, partner. See you tonight."

❦

I DRESSED IN THE REQUESTED ATTIRE AND TOOK THE ELEVATOR down to the fourth floor, ringing the doorbell at unit 405. Mandy had invested in her own preparation. I could smell the scent of bath lotion on her skin. She wore a button-down shirt that flattered the imperfections that embarrassed her. She was barefoot, with plaid-flannel sweatpants completing her ensemble.

Dim lights shed just enough glow to reveal the apartment interior in silhouette. The soundtrack from the film *Garden State* played softly in the background on a laptop computer.

"I love your place," I told her. "Tell me about the pictures."

"That's me before the weight," she said. "I have very few photographs of myself now, on purpose."

I followed her toward the chair and sat. The privacy shades kept prying eyes out, but I could still see the city lights twinkling through them.

"Tell me about that. Tell me about the body shame." I said, trying to draw her out.

"Every girl in my family has the same genome. We're not the anorexics that culture calls sexy. We all have no boobs, were made fun of, and we got the leftovers and the losers as boyfriends."

"That surprises me," I said, even though it didn't.

"It's okay. You don't have to patronize me. I'm paying you. I know why I am who I am. I could have handled it one of two ways: become a comic and make fun of my situation or find someplace where I can hide and get paid."

By now, I knew to envision what might be beneath the exterior and recognize the beauty within. Mandy had potential. I decided that I would at least try to see if she knew it.

"So, how do we do this?" she asked. "Do you want me to start now?"

"It would help me if you undressed, too."

She sniffed. "Help you? I would think it would keep even a professional like yourself from getting it up."

I ignored the self-deprecation. "What are you hiding beneath those clothes?"

"Nothing you would enjoy seeing."

"Let me be the judge of that."

I was close enough to get my hands on her shirt. I released the buttons. She was braless. There wasn't much that needed support. But the other curves were there, some more hidden than others.

With a little care and confidence, Mandy could be a very attractive woman.

Grabbing her hips, I guided her onto my lap. Her legs may have been short, but she was all torso. Her chest was at eye level.

"So," she said. "Are you ready to run away, now that you've seen everything for what it is?"

I slid my thumbs inside the waistband of her sweatpants. "I haven't seen everything. Stand up for a second. If I'm going to be naked, I at least like to have my partner on equal footing."

She didn't stop me. But she turned her head away, suffering, vulnerable. I admired the courage it took to hire me. I intended to over-deliver.

"You'll never get it up now."

I turned her head back toward me.

"Too many people give up on a house when all they see is the front porch." I circled a finger at the center of her chest. "I want to know what's inside that heart."

I put a hand behind her neck and pulled her down to meet my mouth, kissing her softly.

"That's a first," she murmured. "Guys don't want to kiss me. They usually just want me to suck them off."

"And you hired me to reinforce that?"

There was a hint of defiance in her answer. "I'm good at it. One of the best ever. I learned how to please, and watching men enjoy it pleases me."

"Have you ever had sex, Mandy?"

"Who would want to have sex with me?"

"I do. I'm one of the best ever at what I do, too. Start by showing me how good you are, and then I'll show you how good I am. Does that sound fair?"

"I can handle the first part." Her voice trailed off until it was barely a whisper. "But the second part—I don't know how."

I kissed her again. This time she nearly kissed back.

"Great! I'm the perfect guy to teach you."

I leaned back in the chair and opened my robe, pointing toward her interest.

"He's all yours. Show me."

"Do you have anything special you like a woman to do when she gives you oral sex?"

I chuckled. "That's a little clinical."

"Everybody is different. I just want to make sure I do what you like."

"Go with your instincts. I trust you totally."

Mandy displayed the slightest hint of a smile. She lifted my virility up and planted light kisses, beginning at the very top and working her way down. When she got to the base, she took the tip of her tongue and slowly licked me from bottom to top. Her tongue gently tickled my frenulum as she held me in position, waiting for the blood to pump.

I thought of how much there still was to learn about this human being and about the treasures and torments that I might discover. Whatever physical attributes might have been a turnoff fell away, and I could see her aura.

It was hard to explain that without going into new-age stuff, but I guessed it was just another gift I had: the ability to see the energy fields that surround a body. In retrospect, that was what had connected me to Ellen. Yes, at first, her body was a temple to a hormone-charged twenty-one-year-old. But, at that moment, where I felt our genuine connection, I had seen her aura. And damn, how it had turned me on.

Mandy's was a rich mixture of desire, pain, excitement, and shame. It immediately drew me to her, perhaps channeling some of my suffering to generate empathy. Whatever it was, it did the trick. Looking down, I could see that she was pleased with what was happening.

She salivated, licking me as I lengthened until every square centimeter was soaking wet. She circled the ring around my head. I was hard enough now that she could balance me at attention with her thumbs while her index fingers slid up and down the sides of my shaft.

While she did, she moved her tongue to my tip, drawing circles around the opening. I understood why she was confident about her technique.

When she thought I was thick and long enough, she encircled my base with her thumb and index finger, using the remaining three fingers to massage my balls. Her licking became more aggressive, as if I were the most delicious popsicle she'd ever enjoyed.

Periodically, she glanced up at me for feedback. I typically control my emotional connection. You lose your superpowers when it becomes personal. Tonight, I allowed Mandy to see my pleasure, encouraging her and affirming my appreciation.

"You are fantastic, Mandy. Everything you said is true."

"You taste good," she said, between licks. "I got a hint of what might happen later when I circled you on top. It tastes salty. I can't wait to drink it down."

She knew the right words to say, smiling again as she felt a pulsation in response.

With that, she sucked my head, her tongue continuing to dance circles inside. It was as if she were challenging me to lengthen even more with each pull. My hips involuntarily rose toward her as she drew me in.

When she noticed, she drove down on me, taking my full length into her throat like a sword swallower. She held it there for what seemed like ten seconds. The sensation was not unlike the massaging feeling I got when inside a woman at climax. I loved it.

When she pulled back, there was no gagging. She took a deep breath through her nose and continued working on my head, slowly sliding her circular thumb and forefinger up and down my shaft.

Mandy repeated this process, maybe ten times, adding another finger to the pumping motion, until her entire fist was engaged.

As her rhythm quickened, she focused her mouth on the top, tightening her grip with the increase in tempo.

I abandoned any control over my body. When her free hand massaged and lightly slapped my balls, I knew that I was heading toward ejaculation.

Mandy sensed this, thrusting her fist to the bottom of my shaft and grasping it hard as I pumped. She took me into her mouth, sucking me like a milkshake straw. The sounds of her swallowing and the continual tug of her lips intensified my enjoyment.

As I finished, she kept some of my juice in her mouth, rolling it around on her tongue so I could see it, then swallowing one last time with confidence and satisfaction.

"You were right, Mandy," I said, still breathless from this extraordinary experience. "In my world, I have known many women with exquisite oral skills, but nobody comes close."

I lifted her again onto my lap and kissed her, more deeply this time. I could taste myself as I did, concluding our snowballing by twirling my nose against hers in an Eskimo kiss.

"Show me your bedroom," I whispered.

Her face darkened. The fear returned as her self-confidence evaporated.

"Really, David. You don't have to. I got what I paid for."

"I got more than you paid for," I said, planting her on her feet. "Let me do something for you."

She guided me to her bedroom. I knew what rejection felt like. The softness with which she tentatively held my hand was preparation for that eventuality. The harder we try to hold on tight, the more things slip away.

A picture on her dresser revealed the present-day Mandy with her family. Her gene pool was richly diverse. Weight issues seemed to be common, but the faces were warm and genuine.

"You really are attractive when you smile, I said," pointing to the portrait. "You should share that gift with us more often."

Mandy sat on the side of her bed, her hands clasped between her legs as if to protect her treasure chest. I dropped to my knees and looked up at her.

"May I have the honor?"

"David, it's not necessary."

"It's more than just necessary; it's essential," I said, sitting on the carpet and inspecting her.

Mandy's aura was radiating fear and uncertainty.

I knew exactly how to deal with it.

"Let's lie next to one another, so we can talk."

Mandy complied but pulled an afghan over her as I slid beside her.

"A person's physical appearance may fire passion, Mandy, but love lives in the heart. That amazing gift you gave me out there wasn't just an act. I've known women who do it because they are afraid they will lose their man if they don't. Somewhere in your mind, you tied oral sex to acceptance, but along the way, you grew to enjoy the experience. You can't fake that. But it's the only dimension you know well. Let me teach you some others so that when the time comes when you find that person who loves you for what's in your heart, you'll be ready to accept whatever feels good to both of you."

"I've—I've never had sex with anyone," she said.

I wiggled the fingers on my left hand. "Have you known Tom Thumb and his four brothers?"

For the first time, I heard Mandy's laugh. It wasn't the deep diaphragm laugh parodied in cartoons. It was like a mountain stream tumbling over a small waterfall—light, authentic, and attractive.

"Yes. I know that family pretty well."

"Aha! You've got a lot more passion in there than you let on."

I traced the edges of her lips with my finger as I moved closer to her.

"The other stuff is a lot like what you are so good at."

I gave her a light peck on the lips.

"You start gently."

I kissed her neck and her shoulders, then made my move to her modest chest.

"And find the magic points where the wiring connects to what turns you on."

My tongue circled her nipples. I was pleased to see them respond. Mandy couldn't help moaning.

I held my palm just above her warmth, letting it caress the tips of her pubic hair.

Mandy inhaled. The inner vibrations that I knew were a precursor to her sexual peak began.

"And I'm guessing we won't have to work too hard to bring home the goods."

Within the bushes, her passion point emerged, one of the most perfect pearls I could remember.

I brushed against it with my little finger, and she climaxed with such force that the bed shook.

"Holy shit! That was light years better than Mr. Thumb's family," she said.

She was becoming more comfortable with me. Mandy tossed the afghan off of the bed and lay on her back.

"Where do we go from here?"

I put my palms together in a Hindu prayer pose.

"It will be my honor to take you there. How do you feel about oral sex?"

"I would tell you if anyone had ever done it to me."

I crawled back toward the bottom of the bed.

"Pay attention. There will be a test after."

I parted her pubic hair with slow finger motions, reinforcing her confidence with words of affection.

"Butterflies can't see their own wings, so they have no idea how beautiful they are. Some men would die to explore this magic garden."

Mandy took a deep breath and exhaled. The tension lifted. Her visual focus on what I was doing completed the mind-body connection that triggered the best orgasms.

My moves were unhurried and tender as if every centimeter was an acre of diamonds. Monica's teachings were in my mind. It was almost as if her presence was guiding me.

Between my tongue and my fingers, Mandy quickly came twice more, each more powerful than the last.

She put her own hand in the middle of my work zone and felt her wetness.

"Damn, I'm soaked."

She could see my fully piqued interest.

"Let me care for you, Mandy. You deserve it, and I am honored to be the one to do it."

"Screw the 'care for you' stuff," she said in a new, more direct voice. "Just fuck me until my eyeballs fall out. Damn! I've wanted this for years."

She spread her legs and beckoned.

"Fuck me, David. Fuck me so hard that we'll both need to visit a chiropractor when we're done."

I'd heard of the tigresses that often live inside repressed women, pressing at the walls of self-imposed prisons until some event breaks down the walls. Mandy's immense transformation both pleased and stunned me. It was abrupt and unexpected, but I wanted to encourage her, not hinder her. This was her nickel, and I intended to over-deliver.

She had more stamina than I thought possible. Years of suppressed sexual tension swiftly dissipated.

Mandy quickly picked up on every move and every position, challenging me to come and ripping off my condom when I did so she could drink down my production.

We did the deed on her bed, in the living room, on the kitchen counter, on the carpet, and even took a last lap in the bathroom before I had to calm her down so I could head upstairs and get some sleep. Every lap included her own glorious oral contributions.

It wasn't often that I felt exhausted after spending time with a client. Mandy truly had worn me out.

Dressed again in my robe, I stood at her front door. She circled her arms around my waist, her bright eyes glowing.

"You made me feel pretty tonight, David."

"You are beautiful, Mandy," I answered. "I find you incredibly attractive and enjoyed every moment of our time together."

"I would love to become a regular," she said. "If you do that sort of thing."

"I would like that. But you and I both know what the actual goal of this evening was."

Her laughter flowed over me like a waterfall. "To make me consider that I deserve to be loved, to enjoy an endless evening of sex, with someone I'm not paying."

I nodded. "I'm good at what I do. But I always recommend that people include a quality therapist in their circle of advisers. You are a lot more normal than you realize, Mandy. Explore the beauty within. I bet you'll be surprised by what you find."

"But in the meantime, I'd like to buy a season pass to that amazing love muscle of yours."

Mandy reached into my bathrobe and gave it a squeeze.

"Fair enough," I said, backing out of the door and into the hall. "You've got my number."

Mandy leaned against the doorway. She opened her mouth and slid her tongue back and forth across her front teeth.

"I will look forward to tasting you again."

I felt a moment of concern. Client attachment was something new. What had I just created?

When I returned to my condo and checked my pockets for the key fob, I discovered that she had deposited twice the agreed-upon fee.

I could hear Adrian's voice saying, "Okay, big boy. Time to raise the rates."

18

OUR FIRST FIGHT

ELLEN
Well, goddammit to fucking hell. I had just fucked up the best thing that had ever happened to me.

The last two years had been a whirlwind. Corbin Cosmetics was the right idea in the right place at the right time. I had barely put up my shingle, and the talent started seeking me out. I found some fantastic hypoallergenic cosmetic scientists, fragrance chemists, branding, and marketing people, you name it. They shared my vision and enthusiasm.

I needed a lab, and Adrian's people had found one. Everything the team came up with was a hit with our test groups, and soon we were ready to scale. We worked with the city on some incentives and took over an abandoned place in pretty good shape. I threw some money at it to install the latest in manufacturing and packaging technology and created a ton of jobs that made it possible for both some homeless and disabled folks to have careers.

Then one of David's clients took some of my stuff to Europe, a celebrity talked about it on Facebook, and we went off the charts. I couldn't keep up with the demand. Damon and Wade knew the right buttons to push, and we were ahead of schedule. There was so much cash coming in that I started talking about an initial public offering.

Now that Damon was in the picture, the due diligence of that relationship also required time.

I had my hands in everything, and balancing a home life became an issue. David wasn't the problem. He never seemed to be needy, could fly to meet me anywhere, and often did. The cologne I had named after him was soaring off the shelves in London, and I even trotted him out for the Fleet Street gang. Damon knew all about us but was not the least bit jealous. Being associated with my brand didn't hurt David's business, either. But he always paced himself. "Quality, not quantity," he always said.

What had started our fight was Elise. I just didn't have the time to be with her as much as I would have liked. I had hired a nanny. Elise was a possessive four-year-old who loved her mommy. She had huge meltdowns whenever I left, which was often.

David witnessed a few of them and pressed me to hire a COO to manage more of the day-to-day.

"Then you can focus on what you like best," he said. "Creating new things and cuddling with your daughter."

The fact was, I had morphed into a control freak. I thought it was my attention to detail that made the company what it was, and I just couldn't let go. The behavior spilled over into my private life. I wasn't as engaged with Elise's nanny and missed one of her preschool dance performances. That was when David lost it.

"I told you from the start that life wasn't about money!" he said.

"That's easy for you to say. I made your lifestyle possible." I instantly regretted those words. I didn't even mean them.

He became quiet. I knew I was in trouble.

"This isn't about me, Ellen. And it isn't about us. It's about one person and one person only—Elise. I know what it's like to be left alone when you're young. You may not be dead to Elise, but you're becoming invisible. If you care more about showing your ex-husband how you can kick his financial ass than you do about making sure your kid feels loved, your priorities are in the wrong places."

Things went downhill from there. I screamed at him, and he sat there quietly, taking it in and trying to "re-center" me. The calmer he got, the madder I became.

Finally, he stood up and walked toward the door. Maria—Elise's nanny—tried to keep my daughter in the west wing of the house, but my kid knew exactly what was happening and was crying her little eyes out.

She ran into the room just as David was leaving and held onto his leg.

"Please don't go, Uncle D!"

It ripped my heart to shreds.

David leaned down and picked her up so she could be on his level. He was always doing that. Sitting on the floor to make eye contact with her. Lying next to her in bed so she could see his face as he talked with her. He wanted her to feel like she was his equal.

"I'm always here for you, chipmunk. If you ever need me, tell Maria, and I'll be right here."

"I want you here *now*, Uncle D."

"Your mom needs her space right now, baby. We'll talk later."

He kissed her forehead and handed her to the nanny as Elise wailed again.

David smiled at them. He fucking smiled at them in the middle of this tremendous fight.

"You know my number, Maria. I love you both."

And then he was gone.

Holy fucking shit cakes on a pogo stick. I was so mad. David was the one who had encouraged me to chase the dream. He did whatever I asked to support it. And now, when the IPO was about to drop and the British plant was about to open another wing, he fucking walked out.

That put me over the edge. I started circling the kitchen, throwing things against the wall. Pots and pans, glasses, dishes, anything I saw. I was cursing him, screaming my guts out.

Suddenly some movement caught my eye. Maria and Elise were standing in the doorway. The nanny's mouth was hanging open. Elise was holding onto her hand, sobbing and covering her eyes.

"Mommy, stop. Mommy, stop. Mommy, stop." She kept saying

that over and over, making the gasping sound she made when she cried so hard she couldn't catch her breath.

I took the BMW keys and bolted. I left my child crying in her nanny's arms and ran away. I couldn't go to the office because my face was such a mess, and I didn't want the employees to see me looking like a weak female. I realized that I had been so single-minded about the business that the friends who surrounded me that wonderful New Year's Eve two years ago had drifted away. Or had I drifted away from them? There was nowhere I could go.

I just drove, barely able to see through my tears.

I tried to focus on the to-do list in my head but couldn't. My eyes caught a picture that hung from the visor. David, Elise, and me on the beach at Lake Michigan.

❦

THE PREVIOUS SUMMER WAS ONE OF THE WARMEST IN MEMORY. Corbin Cosmetics was a thing, but not yet an all-consuming obsession. David found a cottage near Saugatuck. It perched on a bluff with a perfect panorama of the ice-blue water. The three of us took long beach walks every morning, stopping whenever Elise found some shells or a piece of driftwood and dashing into the surf whenever the sun felt too hot.

At the dawn of her precociousness, my daughter was full of questions that she spouted with her newly acquired toolbox of words. She was beginning to figure out that her little friends in the neighborhood had both mothers and fathers and was trying to make sense of our unique relationship.

"What happened to my daddy?" she asked, focused on the circular patterns of a Petoskey stone David had found.

I had practiced for this inevitable conversation, but my words still felt awkward. "Sometimes moms and dads decide that it's better for their kids if they don't live together," I said.

"Is that di–divorce?"

I nodded. Elise was still looking at her treasure, but I knew she was paying attention to me. "Yes, baby. Divorce is when two people decide that they don't want to be married anymore."

"Is Daddy a bad man?"

"No, honey, he isn't," I lied. "Our lives just grew in different directions."

"I'm glad," Elise said. She turned her gaze to David. "Because now we have Uncle D."

David smiled and rubbed her head. "I'm glad, too, chipmunk. I really like being with you and your mom."

"Then why don't you marry mommy, Uncle D?"

David looked over at me to see if I wanted to answer that one. I pressed my lips together, scrunching my eyebrows into an embarrassed confusion. David smiled.

"When two people care about each other, they don't always need to be married. Rings and churches and white dresses are fun. But being married is something that starts in your heart. It's like how you feel when Mom tucks you in on Christmas eve. You know that good things are going to happen and you can't wait to see what they are."

Elise wasn't buying it. "I want you to marry Mommy."

David crouched down so he could look my daughter in the eye. "Yeah? Why?"

"Because I want you to be my daddy."

He picked her up and spun her around in his arms. "I'm always here for you, chipmunk. Don't ever worry about that."

🍂

JESUS FUCKING CHRIST AND HIS ALL-GIRL ORCHESTRA. WHAT IN the hell was I doing? David was right. Operations is a science. I could hire outstanding talent to manage that. I was the creator, the visionary, the dreamer. The brand had my name on it because I wanted to help make other people feel better about themselves. My entire marketing message was about "Bringing the Beauty Inside Out."

The person I was becoming was the opposite of everything I believed in.

I looked in the mirror over the dresser and saw Brad's face. I was becoming him, and I hated it. That wasn't who I was.

And then I remembered something else.

David and I were at a bar about eight months after he had started grad school. One of his former co-workers sauntered up to our table.

"You know, you never bought me that drink, David," he said.

There was a strange expression on David's face, like someone close to us was about to tell an embarrassing story.

"Wait here," he said. "What are you drinking?"

"None of that Coca-Cola kids' stuff you're drinking, ya big wimp. Go get me a dirty martini."

David left, and his friend took a stool across from me.

His smart-ass demeanor softened. He offered me a hand.

"I'm Jerry . . . He never told you, did he?"

"Told me what?"

"What he did that day he met you when he said there was a problem with the wiring."

"What are you talking about?"

"David found out you owed the cable company over four hundred bucks. He took out his nearly maxed-out credit card and insisted on paying it off. I ended up helping him a little, and he promised me a beer for my trouble. Now that he's making way more money than I ever will, I called the marker."

"Are you saying I owed you money, and David took care of it?"

"We took care of it, ma'am. It was a bit of a team effort. But I wanted you to know what kind of guy you have looking out for you."

David was heading back from the bar with the martini.

"And don't you dare tell him I told you!"

That did it. I turned back the pages of my diary to read my entry from the morning after Adrian and I had fucked David's lights out.

"Surround yourself with good people," I had told him. "Tell them what you need. Give them the support to be able to be successful. And every problem will ultimately take care of itself."

I had given David my success mantra. He had practiced it to the letter and had become the wonderful person I couldn't imagine living without.

And I wasn't even following it myself.

I sent David a text.

Me: I'm calmer now.

Me: Can we talk?

David: Meet me at 3480 Spring St.

In my state, the address had no meaning. I did not understand what he was talking about. But I texted back that I would be there in twenty minutes.

I did what I could to put my face back together. Women hate to cry because it makes our eyes get puffy, and people can tell. Looking good was now my business, and there was no way I could cover that up. My creative mind resolved to ponder that one.

The door to 3480 Spring Street was open as I pulled into the driveway. My memory finally made the connection.

This was the house where we had met. In my maelstrom of shame, I had banished every memory of that place, save one.

David's car was in the driveway. I pulled in behind him so he couldn't ditch me and walked inside.

Never have I felt so afraid.

The place was in much better condition than when Elise and I had lived here. Someone had given it tender, loving care, from the new insulated windows to the shiny appliances in the small kitchen. This was no longer a rental. Fresh paint and carpet gave the place a new-home feel. I recognized two furniture pieces as survivors from my brief time as a tenant.

It was getting dark now. There was one light on—the bedroom where David and I had forever changed one another's lives.

The bed was a better fit, a queen, not the king that had nearly filled every square inch of the place.

David was sitting on the edge of the bed. He was smiling at me.

"How did you get permission to be here?"

Yeah, that was the best opening line I could come up with. Pathetic.

"It's ours, Ellen. I bought it."

"But why?"

"It's where we began. You know I won't ever tell you how to live your life. But I never want to forget how you changed mine. I bought this with my bonus money in January. I come here when I feel like I'm losing my way. The deed is in both of our names. It's here for you, too. Maybe someday, Elise might want to call it home. It will always be home to me."

David stood. The love in his eyes was tinged with sadness. I had hurt him deeply. But somehow, his heart was still open. He still cared when most people would have walked out, intending never to come back. The abandonment issues from the divorce washed over me, leaving my body cold and fearful.

"Do what you need to do, Ellen. But no matter what you do, I will still love you."

I fell into his arms and sobbed. So much for the makeup. David gently guided me to the bed and put my head on his chest as I wept. It was like that first day but with one difference. My tears then were anger and helplessness. Today they were all about regret.

"I was screaming at you," I said when I finally gained back a modicum of self-control. "Why didn't you scream back? I deserved it."

"Oh, I wanted to. But I also wanted Elise to know how people who love each other can sometimes be angry with each other. She needs to understand that one partner has to keep it together when the other one loses it."

"Would you have screamed back if she hadn't been there?"

David's face projected wisdom way beyond his years.

"Nope. You needed to process all of this in your own way. What you needed most from me was to listen and to try to frame your words in a calmer context."

"I'm recruiting a COO tomorrow," I said.

"If that's what you want to do, I support it. My one concern is that you and Elise have quality time together."

It was a moment of realization for me. I truly loved this man. The age barrier seemed to crumble. Any romantic thoughts I might have entertained about Damon disappeared. I imagined us as life partners. It frightened me, and I didn't know why. I wanted to know how he felt.

"What am I to you, David?"

He looked wistful. "Many things. The role I love most is that you're my best friend."

"Even after what I said back at the house?"

David rubbed the teardrops from beneath my eyes with his thumbs. We were so close that I could smell his scent. I had bottled that scent, and it was making me millions. I felt my love button swell. I wanted him so badly—physically, intellectually, and spiritually.

He whispered those words in my ear, "No matter what you do, I will still love you."

I literally tore off his clothes and ripped a section of my own two-thousand-dollar Versace outfit from my body. Seeing him spring free as I pulled off his pants brought a wave of relief.

The words he said weren't just lyrics in some song. He meant them.

I went down on him, feeling myself losing control.

He stopped me.

"This way," he said, bringing me again to his side. "We're equals."

I felt a gush of wetness flow from inside me. I took hold of the object of my affection, applying the protection that was our habit and rubbing it against my pulsing sex before slowly welcoming him into me.

My desire was overpowering.

"I know we're equals. But please get on top of me and fuck me until I come to my senses. I know that's what you really want. And it's definitely what I want."

The beautiful eyes I knew so well confirmed that I was right.

I rolled him onto me and swung my legs over his shoulders so he could press them against me and get the deepest penetration while we kissed.

I knew that somewhere inside, David must have been repressing the anger and aggression that would be natural reactions to my behavior. I was determined to get it out of him.

"Harder, baby. Harder. Please don't be calm. Please. Please pound me. Harder. Deeper."

My urging was doing the trick. The control David was becoming famous for was gone. I was the one in control now. I felt a combination of satisfaction and uncertainty. I had disappointed David today. Now I had his heart in my hands.

David devoured me like a thirsty man lost in the desert. I giggled and whimpered as he pulled my nipple deep into his mouth. I could hear him moaning as his pumping down below became harder and faster.

Normally, I would have totally climaxed by now. But I had learned a lesson about caring for others, too. While my insides quivered, begging me to let them come, I held back, waiting for my love to reach his own orgasm.

David suddenly arched, and I finally allowed myself to go over the edge with him.

My entire body shook as David pressed a final thrust and held himself deep inside of me.

I wanted to remember that moment. I was grateful it took place where we had first found one another.

Wrapping my legs around David's back, I covered his face with kisses.

"I'm so sorry, my love. I'm so, so sorry. Thank you for bringing me back to my center. And thank you for allowing me to feel some anger that must have been in your own heart as you fucked me."

"You don't have to apologize for strong convictions, Ellen." My handsome lover was so exhausted. He was panting the words. "Women vector to 'I'm sorry' so easily. And it wasn't about me at all. My singular concern was Elise. I lost my parents. I don't want her to lose her wonderful mother."

David was spent. His head laid limp against my shoulder. He tried to embrace me, but I had sucked all the energy out of him.

Sucked...

There was one thing more I wanted to do.

I rolled David over onto his back.

He could barely raise his head.

"I don't know if I have any more to give you, Ellen,"

"Just relax and breathe, my love. I'll take care of everything."

David had described his experience with Mandy in great detail. I knew that talking about our escapades sounded like a kink in itself, but that was how open we were with one another about sexuality. His tales of her oral prowess fascinated me. I wanted to see if I could recreate the experience.

The moment David realized what I was doing, I could see the heartbeats pulsing on either side of his neck increase. The gorgeous pectorals on his chest tightened.

He took a deep breath, exhaling, in what I knew was his way of centering his mind and releasing his stress. He closed his eyes, nodding and smiling as I copied Mandy's every move. I felt my own excitement rising as he thickened in my fist. When I tasted the first hint of his precum, I was wet again, my insides vibrating in anticipation.

But this was all about him.

"Thank you for loving me," I said as I gulped in air after taking his full measure down my throat.

Our gazes locked. I dove on him again, sensing the nearness of his climax. His hips began to move up and down in sync with my advances.

"Come for me. Feed me. Fill my mouth. Please. Please."

Our many erotic experiences sharpened my sense of exactly how to bring my lover to climax. David's was wonderful. He groaned as he arched up toward me. I held him in both hands, my mouth over his head, and pulled in tandem with the gushes of white liquid that he gave to me with every lunge.

I closed my eyes to enjoy it. And then his experienced fingers tickled my gem. Two more slid inside of me. I came like it was the Fourth of July, "Rockets' red glare" and all, shaking as I continued to suck down David's milk.

I lay next to my love on the bed in the same room where our adventures had begun. Now I knew the things I wanted to tell him. I couldn't let go of the failure of my marriage. It was pure parental approval stuff that was driving me to outdo Brad in every arena.

David had pulled me back from the danger zone, and all he had done was care about me.

And then there was Damon. My trips to England were more frequent. And not just because there was business to tend to. I found myself falling for Damon. He treated me like a queen, added incredible value to the company and wooed me with so many "David behaviors" that I sometimes thought Damon was an older version of my perfect man.

The one thing both David and I hoped I would find. How would he react when I confessed my feelings for Damon?

I gathered all the courage I could muster and thought of how to put my feelings into words.

But as I was about to begin, he put a finger on my lips.

"We should get cleaned up," he said. "Elise is waiting for you at your parents' place. Let's go pick her up together."

❧ 19 ❧

EVA

DAVID

Ellen quickly became one of the most well-known names in her industry. Her personality and her backstory were the stuff of pop culture heaven. That she would attract followers was inevitable.

And though we had a unique relationship, I still hoped she might find a more traditional partner. Damon Winslow seemed to fit the bill. Our fight and the emotional reconciliation felt like signs that perhaps what Ellen needed was someone closer to her own emerging world.

It may sound strange to have such a passionate connection with somebody and still want them to seek their definition of happiness, even if that meant loving someone else. Talking the talk was easy. Could I walk the walk?

We had always kept separate accommodations, even when we traveled together. And although I almost always ended up sleeping next to Ellen, just knowing there was space if we needed it was an important dimension of our relationship.

So, I guessed I wasn't surprised one morning when she told me that her thing with Damon was progressing. In my usual Saturday position, I was on the floor playing with Elise, while Ellen was studying the week's stock market activity on her laptop.

"I'm feeling a connection with this guy." She tried to make it sound casual.

I knew her well enough to sense her nervousness.

I hoped I could sell mine better than she was selling hers. "Tell me more."

"He's been involved with two start-ups. Never married. Likes kids. Self-made. A lot like you, David, just a bit closer to my age."

I knew exactly who she was talking about. Adrian had warned me.

"I like him already," I lied.

"I think I like him, too. He's been helping me with this mountain of SEC paperwork connected to the IPO."

"What do you like best about him?"

"He's a free spirit, just like you."

"And?"

"It feels like he is ready to pull back a bit from the grind and enjoy life. That's a wonderful compliment for a hard charger like me who needs to learn to live a little."

"Are we talking about Damon?"

A tinge of embarrassment colored Ellen's cheeks. "Yes. The British guy."

I picked Elise up and walked over to the kitchen island, where Ellen perched with her laptop.

"What do we think, Elise? Do we want Momma to be happy?"

"Yes, we do," her tiny voice said. She nuzzled my ear with her nose. "Just like you make her happy, Uncle D."

I laughed, trying not to make it sound nervous. "I think this is a different kind of happiness, Elise. But just as important."

"I like happy," Elise said. "Any happy is good happy." There wasn't the uncomfortable moment I expected. Elise seemed to have forgotten our conversation on the beach. Or perhaps she was just focused on playing.

She wiggled out of my arms and ran back to her pile of blocks.

I was getting my act down now. The thought of what I might lose had never crossed my mind until that moment. The bilious taste of terror bubbled up from my stomach and into my throat. My heart was pounding. But I kept my cool. "Sounds like consensus to me."

Ellen gave me one of her serious looks.

"Are you really okay with the idea?"

"All I've ever wanted is for you to find your definition of happiness. Just make sure he knows there's a guy out there who will beat the shit out of him if he breaks your heart."

I put my hand on hers. They were trembling.

I winked at Ellen and went back to Elise and her blocks, aware that she watched us both very closely.

⁂

I GUESS IT WAS ALSO INEVITABLE THAT I WOULD EVENTUALLY MEET an opposite number in my unique profession. That same night, 1 was escorting Patricia, one of my regulars, to a professional function where she was speaking. I stood in the back of the room, sipping my Coke as the emcee, a billionaire, made the introduction.

A woman I judged to be about Ellen's age slid next to me.

"Working tonight, too?"

She was a knockout. Five-nine, about one-twenty-five, flawlessly proportioned, carefully colored auburn hair, brown eyes, lots of jewelry, no wedding ring. Her top swooped down a little deeper than a wife might dare.

I offered a hand. "I'm with Patricia. David. David Orion."

She took it, allowing me to put my other hand on top of hers as I held it.

"Eva St. Claire. I know all about you." She pointed to the emcee. "John. That's my date. He told me you take care of Patty's 'special needs.'"

"John?"

"John, the guy who is introducing her up there. He trots me out whenever he needs an appropriate accouterment for events like these."

She had the slightest hint of a Latin accent. I chuckled as I thought about how she defined us. "Accoutrements. I've never been called that before."

She turned to me, straightening my black bow tie. "So, I guess I should ask you a shop-talk question like, how's business?"

"You're suggesting that we ply the same trade?"

"We're hookers, David. Well paid and proud purveyors of the world's oldest profession."

It wasn't how I defined myself, but she had a point.

"I see it a bit differently, Eva, but that's pretty much what we do."

John finished his introduction, and Patricia got the requisite standing ovation. John sat on the dais with the rest of the important people as she began her remarks. I knew them by heart and had even written some of the speech for her.

Eva bumped my waist with her hip. "Wanna get out of here and sit at the bar? This is going to be boring."

I gave her a conspiratorial nod, and we edged quietly out of the room.

"I guess if there's a traditional route that women follow into the trade, I took it," Eva said when we comfortably ensconced in a booth by the bar. "Worked in the family business as a kid. Got into porn after high school. Had a profitable run for about ten years. Then, I learned about this escort thing and have been making good money ever since."

I asked the question that was troubling my own subconscious mind. "How much longer do you want to keep working?"

"What? I'm only thirty-five. Are you saying I look older than my years?"

"Not at all. I'm a finance guy in the daytime. I get paid to look over the horizon."

Eva smirked, unoffended. She was messing with my head.

"It's not as much fun as it used to be. I feel like I'm going through the motions. But I didn't understand money until I spent most of it. I'll probably do this as long as there are men who will do me. I won't die a rich woman."

"Ever been in love?"

Eva raised an eyebrow. "Wow, you ask the questions, don't you?

Yeah, at least I thought so. A couple of times. The guys I attract aren't interested in my personality. Enough about me, David. What's your story?"

"My thing just kind of happened. Before I knew it, I had this referral business and I could barely keep up. I'm particular now. Most of my clients hire me because they are lonely or have body issues or low self-esteem. I try to help them understand that genuine beauty is on the inside."

"Yeah, right." Eva's voice dripped with sarcasm. "Most guys can't wait to get inside me. They want to bang every orifice, and then they come, and they go."

I tried a variation of my question on her. "What would make you happy, Eva?"

A person's face tells me a lot about what is going on in their minds. Hers was wistful; the eyes focused on some infinite point where her answers might be. The rapid movement of her pupils seemed to replay a plethora of past memories, definitely with regrets.

"I sometimes wonder what would have happened if I did the wife and kids thing. But with my luck, I'd probably end up a single mom with babies who grew up to be gang bangers."

"No, really. Have you thought about it?"

"All the time. But what can a person with my resume do? Once you are what you are in my business, you can't change your life. I just hope I can find somebody who will like me enough to take care of me when I can't spread my legs anymore."

I wondered about the new man in Ellen's life. Did his free spirit include caring for her as the pages of time turned? Was Adrian's assessment that Damon was an opportunist valid? We had not yet met, but my own investigations were revealing troubling pictures of a man with a spirit that was a little too free and a taste of a lifestyle that he might not be able to maintain without help.

Eva signaled to our waitress for a refill. "You don't drink?"

"I like being able to remember things."

When her drink arrived, Eva downed it in a single gulp.

"I like to forget things."

I could hear Patricia concluding her remarks in the next room. It was time to go back to work. I paid the bar bill and wrapped my two hands around hers.

"Well, I'm glad to have met you, Eva. It sounds like you've done more than just be a survivor. I hope that someday you will figure out what your definition of happiness is and chase it."

"You seem like a decent guy, David. Give me your card. I may have some business for you in the future."

I held her chair as she stood, handed her a business card, and opened the conference room door for her as Patricia's applause swelled.

"A gentleman," Eva said. "So rare. And so appreciated."

It turned out that Patricia was invited to an afterglow gathering and didn't need my support anymore that night. I kissed her cheek, and she slipped an envelope with my fee into the pocket of my sport coat. "I wish I didn't have to do this damn thing. I'd rather be in your arms."

I knew she meant it. "Me too, Patricia. Until next time."

I was headed to the valet when someone pinched my rear end.

"Hey, big boy. Want to compare techniques?"

Apparently, John no longer needed Eva's services tonight, either.

"Eva. We meet again so soon."

"I've got my own suite upstairs. Care to join me to continue the happiness conversation?"

I was tired, still trying to wrap my head around the news of Ellen's progressing relationship. The jacuzzi jets of the condo bathtub were calling me.

"It's a generous offer, but I'm ready to relax in my own space."

Eva pulled me to the side of the hallway. Her hand went into her bra, and out came a wad of cash. She started peeling off one-hundred-dollar bills.

"Tell me when to stop."

"Look, Eva—"

She crammed the entire wad into my pants pocket, fucking me with her eyes in the process.

"My entire take tonight. I've heard about your talents. Give me a little demonstration, and I'll return the favor."

Eva would not be denied.

I took the money out of my pocket and put it back into her hands.

"Okay, kiddo. But let's consider this professional courtesy. I'm not your customer, and you're not my client. If you're up for being yourself and just talking, I'll hang with you for a bit."

John had set up Eva with the hotel's best suite. Holding the door for her, I could see champagne and flowers on a glass table in the living room. The housekeeping staff had set the mood lighting appropriately. Soft music was whispering from speakers in the ceiling while mountain scenes played on the huge flat-screen TV.

Eva waved a hand to take it all in. "This is what a blow job and some anal gets you if you're a girl with tits and skills."

I found a single leather chair and sank into it. Eva handed me a Coke from the generously stocked minibar. I pointed to the champagne.

"Want me to pop the cork for you?"

She shook her head, holding up a bottle of Rémy Martin XO. "My, aren't we forward? Shouldn't we get to know one another better first?"

I took a swallow of my soda, hoping the caffeine might get me out of the funk that was slowly enveloping me. I had convinced Ellen to prioritize Elise. It was becoming clear how much I wished she would prioritize me.

Eva unbuttoned her blouse. "Do you mind? I prefer T-shirts and sweatpants when I'm off duty."

I stood, offering to step outside for a few moments. "Would you like some privacy?"

"Oh, God! Like you and the world haven't seen me naked."

I had not; I admitted it to her.

She was incredulous. "You're not that old. You can't tell me you've never jerked off to one of my many video performances."

"I'm afraid I didn't know who you were until we met downstairs tonight, Eva. And not because I haven't jerked off. I was just like any other kid. I did my share of self-fulfillment."

Eva shrugged. "I thought I was a bigger star."

She unhooked her bra, revealing a pair of massive breasts. They showed the signs of a plastic surgeon's art. Whoever she used wasn't the five-star variety.

Eva saw me inspecting her. "Fucking doctor. He screwed up my last implant procedure. I have a malpractice case working its way through the courts. If that pays off, I'll definitely be retiring."

"How do you hide something like that?" I asked.

"You don't. For some guys, scars are a turn-on. Sick fucks. But these vertical mutilations pretty much ended my film career."

I thought about several clients who were cancer survivors. They were some of the most courageous and passionate women I had known. I found them appealing, even with twin scars and emptiness where their breasts used to be.

But they didn't depend on their chests to make their living like Eva did.

She dropped her skirt to the floor, revealing a thong that barely creased her nether regions.

A pair of baggy flannel pajama pants with red hearts on a white background soon covered it. Eva completed the ensemble with a thin cotton T-shirt that left little to the imagination. A professional sports team logo adorned the center.

"I used to be their mascot. Fucked the entire team, the trainers, the head coach."

"Do you even enjoy sex anymore, Eva?" I asked.

"What the fuck, David? Are you a shrink or something? Of course, I don't. It's just a predictable pattern of moves that I've done thousands of times, including some of the most convincing moans that ever made a teenager cream in his jeans."

I felt depressed. Was this what was ahead for me? It couldn't be. My goal was to have a positive impact on as many clients as possible. I ran through my mental address book, thinking about where each client's head was at when I had met her and where it was today. Most seemed better for having crossed my path. But was I rationalizing?

"I guess I approach my work a little differently. I try to leave a client in a better emotional space than I found her."

Eva put her cognac bottle and an ice bucket on the table. She flopped into a chair opposite me. The Remy splashed into the glass, followed by two ice cubes. Eva took a dose.

"A better emotional state? If you could do that for me, I'd give you a year's income. What's your drill?"

"I try to get to know a client a bit before we transact any business and then, I ask them, 'How can I make you happy?' or sometimes, just 'How can I please you?'"

"That second question is a fuck me question. The first one—" Eva thought for a moment. "The first one is sometimes impossible."

"What is your opener?" I wondered.

"'How would you like me to fuck you?' We definitely live in different worlds, David."

I was not liking either of our worlds right now. The magnitude of what was happening in my own life required some contemplation. I wanted to graciously disengage and get out of there.

"Have you thought any more about the happiness question?"

Eva took another pull of her cognac, leaning her head back into the cool, thick leather. "That's all I've been thinking about since you asked me. I have no fucking idea."

"Ever been in therapy?"

"Many times. I may hold the world's record for being fired by shrinks."

"That happens when you won't do the work."

"Bingo! Right on, brother. Spoken like someone else who got the 'termination of treatment' phone call. I don't like doing the work."

I thought about Monica, about how long it had been since she had climaxed and what I was able to do to take her there. I thought about Mandy's transformation from a sexual introvert to a barely caged tiger. A small tingle in my pleasure center made me wonder if I could do that for Eva. I grasped at what I was good at. Perhaps it could give me the courage to do the things I wasn't so good at.

"When was the last time you came? I mean, really came. An authentic, world-class orgasm?"

Eva sucked down the rest of her drink, refilling it from the bottle. "I'd like you to answer that one first."

"Yesterday."

"You have a girlfriend?"

Was that what Ellen was? Now that Damon was in the picture?

I knew what word I wanted to say, but as I thought it, I felt an arrow pierce my heart. "I have a . . . soulmate."

"Good for you. How does she feel about you fucking other women?"

"She helped me create my profession. She's my biggest supporter."

I became conscious of the fact that I was living a double standard. Ellen encouraged me to engage with any woman I wanted. But her announcement that she was interested in someone else was bothering me. And not once had I even explored true intimacy outside of our relationship.

Eva knew none of this, yet.

"Sounds like a marriage made in heaven," she said. "How do you make a woman come? I'm talking about the tough ones who are closed up so tight that they can't begin to approach it."

"I try to get them to see themselves as I see them. Most of my clients have such a horrible self-image that they have no idea how valuable they really are."

"Valuable? Not beautiful?"

I tried hard to come up with an analogy that Eva could comprehend.

"There are probably thousands of men out there who still see you as the gold standard. Yes, you've perfected the act, but in their minds, you epitomize sensuality and magnetism. I've consumed my share of porn, and I can tell who has the goods and who doesn't. For you to have had the career you've enjoyed, there has to be something real behind the performance. You have to have known what it feels like to be so attracted to someone that you give everything that's in your heart when you love them."

"Not really. I could fuck you right here, right now, and you would be absolutely certain that you made me come like a thunderbolt, while in my head, I'm thinking about binge-watching Netflix."

I felt pity for this woman. She was so insulated from feeling anything that her life was nothing more than going through the motions. But how to say it to her productively?

"I'm struggling, Eva. There is so much I want to say to you, but I don't know how to say it."

"Try being direct. It will be a pleasant surprise to get honesty from a man."

"Okay. I'll try. We're all damaged goods. Along the way, people or events have screwed us up. We learn skills to cope, to survive. Sometimes those very skills numb us to the work we really need to do to heal. You have built your personality, your physical body, around survival in a business that objectifies you. You have so many shields up that not even the important stuff can break them down. Every time you see a guy naked, it's 'here we go again; how do I get through this?' You've done what you needed to do, Eva, not just to survive but to enter the upper reaches of your profession. What breaks my heart is that you sacrificed your vulnerability in the process."

"It's a fuck or get fucked world, David. I'm surprised you, of all people, haven't realized that yet."

I shook my head. "That's not totally true. Yes, we have to protect ourselves from the bad people out there. But we also have to be willing to risk our own hearts from time to time, to trust that the universe will give us what we need to find our own way to our purpose. Happiness follows purpose, Eva. But not if it's so narrow that all that defines it is just getting through the day."

Eva's face darkened. "Every time I've opened my heart, it's been stomped on."

How much truth could Eva take?

I didn't really know this woman. It was late. I was tired.

"Perhaps you haven't opened it to the right person."

Eva was silent. Her hands intertwined, index fingers pointed upward, touching her lips again and again as she thought. There was nothing to do but wait to see what might happen next.

After a time, she lifted the cognac glass, studying it as if it were a prism. She put it down and pushed it away, turning to face me.

The swagger and the cynicism were gone. She seemed as fragile as a porcelain doll. "What does a good person look like?"

"A good person cherishes you for the precious treasure that you are. He realizes you are imperfect and loves you anyway. He is as drawn to your mind as he is to your body. He acknowledges your right to be angry, comforts you when you are sad, helps heal you when you feel broken. Sometimes he just listens. He celebrates your independence and prioritizes the endurance of the partnership above the individuals in it. He compliments you when he's proud of you and calls you out when you step over the line. He never stops doing the little things that made you love him in the first place. Most of all, he wants your happiness, even if that means it's ultimately with somebody else."

I caught "the look." Her armor was coming down. She was sizing me up in a different way, the way that my clients did when we were about to move into the bedroom.

"Where would I find such a man?"

"You'll know him when you see him, Eva. It likely won't be that thunderbolt you described. True love sneaks up on you. You don't realize you're in it until it's already a done deal."

In that instant, I knew. Love had snuck up on me. And I was so attached to this stupid age-difference thing I had convinced myself that Ellen could do better. Could I?

Eva leaned toward me. Her chest pressed against the front of her T-shirt as her nipples hardened.

"I see why you do so well with women, David. I think you are exactly the man you describe."

She was speaking from the heart, maybe for the first time in years.

"I hope your soulmate realizes what she's got."

I knew what I had. And what might now be at risk. I heard myself saying things to Eva that I never thought I would say.

"She's falling for someone else. We have this open relationship. She encourages me to do what I do. This is the first time she's ever mentioned being interested in anybody besides me. I've always wanted her happiness. But I'm afraid, Eva. I'm afraid of losing her."

Eva's stare pierced me. I could no longer read what was behind it.

"You're making me wet, David. That hasn't happened without lube in ten years. That thing you said about wanting the other person to be happy, even if it was with someone else. Do you believe that?"

"I thought I did. I want to. It was so easy when there wasn't any real threat. Suddenly it isn't easy at all."

Eva moved closer, sitting on the edge of the glass table, our knees touching. She took my hands in hers.

"I guess you are just going to prove your theory by trusting the universe."

My own words coming back at me. I had to admit the irony. "There's really no other choice, is there?"

"Nope. And I'll tell you something else. I've fucked people for a living my entire adult life. Sex has become nothing more than a business transaction for me. But right now? You are the first person I've ever desired."

"Ahh. So, you know the difference, after all."

Eva smiled. It was a sad smile that communicated wisdom born of pain. "Yes. Thank you for being vulnerable, David. You are reminding me how it's done."

Her thumbs were massaging my hands as she held them.

"I feel like I'm taking advantage of you when I ask you this," she said. "But I think a good long fuck is what we both need."

My entire world seemed to spin out of control. Before me was a woman who was much wiser than I had imagined, taking the responsibility and the risk of beginning to heal. I could play a role in that healing at this very moment. But I couldn't get the thought of losing Ellen out of my head.

Eva gently pulled me closer. Her physical perfection was overpowering. And now, I knew a bit of the struggle in her heart. But I felt lost. For the first time, I didn't know what to do.

"You need this as much as I do, sweetheart. And who knows?"

she cocked her head toward the bed. "We might be able to teach each other something new over there."

My willpower was nonexistent. My self-discipline vanished. I stood to follow her, visibly swelling. Ready. Hungry. I wanted her. It made no sense. I was in love with Ellen, but my desire for this woman was off the charts. Was I sublimating my own needs so deeply in every other dimension of my life that now they were bursting to the surface? My famous self-control was gone. My mind slipped into autopilot with one goal. I wanted to fuck Eva senseless.

I didn't remove her clothing at first. I just whispered, "Close your eyes and imagine your perfect man." I began to lightly kiss her neck. "Imagine that the man I described is here with you now. His one focus is on your happiness, and he would do anything to help you find it. Imagine that you are strong and tender. You are will and compassion. Imagine someone who sees past your perfect exterior, who is utterly in love with your imperfect interior. Imagine that he is standing before you right now. His desire to express the love for you that burns in his heart is so strong that his fingers are on fire. They are so sensitive that just gently caressing your face makes him rock hard for you."

I saw the pulsing arteries in Eva's neck quicken. Her right hand reflexively slid beneath her pants and started circling. As I slipped out of my clothing and it slid to the floor, her fingers quickened their pace.

"Jesus Christ," she gasped, "I'm already so fucking close."

I brushed my lips against hers and grazed the tips of her nipples through the cotton that still covered them.

"It's okay, Eva. Let yourself go. You don't need anybody else to validate your worthiness. Beneath that exterior is a wonderful human being, fascinating, admirable, and exquisitely attractive in so many ways."

Eva suddenly threw her body onto the bed, spreading her legs and jamming her fingers inside her. I could hear a series of short inhalations, punctuated by a colossal moan that seemed to erupt from deep within her. Eva's chin vibrated as her hips involuntarily rose toward the hand that was sliding in and out of her slick folds.

As she peaked, Eva began to pant.

"Holy. Shit. Oh. My. God."

I had seen nothing like it.

I ripped off her sweatpants. I gripped her legs, pulling her to the edge of the bed. I couldn't remember ever being as hard or as willing. I slid into her under her fingers and began to pound her.

Eva pulled her T-shirt over her head in a single, cross-armed motion, revealing an undulating chest that amplified my helpless yearning. She moved her hand back to her trigger and started circling it again. Her powerful legs worked in perfect time with my own.

"Deeper. Deeper. Harder. Please."

Her voice was earnest, genuine, pleading. This was no act.

I could do nothing except comply. I channeled my fear, my sadness, and a grief I had not felt since losing my parents into every lunge.

Eva's enhanced breasts rolled back and forth like beach balls on her chest. Her nipples seemed to stand out nearly an inch. I suddenly wanted them in my mouth. But my hips refused to comply.

Her eyes were open now, and she was watching. I could hear myself howl with every thrust. There was satisfaction on her face. She urged me on, still spinning her fingers like a top over the source of her pleasure.

Her climactic clinch was way beyond anything I had known. Eva's rippling inner muscles drew me more deeply into her as she came for a second time.

My own orgasm began. I realized, in horror, that I wasn't wearing a condom.

It was too late.

Blast after blast filled her. I didn't even have the will to pull out, falling forward into her arms as my pumping vesicles continued to empty into her.

I wept, strong, gasping sobs, broken by the contorted inhalations I remembered from my childhood tears.

Eva held me lovingly. Her embrace kept me steady, but it didn't feel like the grasp of someone who was afraid to let go. A tender hand caressed my back, her inner muscles massaging me as I cried. I wanted so much to become flaccid. But I couldn't.

"It's okay, baby," she said. "You made me come twice after I almost forgot what that felt like. Let me take care of you."

Eva rolled me onto my back. She sat on top of me, her thigh muscles slowly sliding me in and out.

"Protection." My voice was hoarse. Unrecognizable. "I'm not wearing any protection for you."

"Don't worry about that, sweetheart. I promise you we are both totally safe. The reason you are still hard is that you still have more to work out. Trust me, as I have trusted you. Let me begin to heal you, too."

Eva leaned toward me, putting her hands on either side of my head.

"I saw you admiring my nipples. Take them. Taste them now."

Through my tears, my tongue found them. It was almost like a French kiss. I still had no control over my desire. However, my movements were surprisingly sensitive, and I could hear Eva groaning in a way that made me even harder.

"The tits may be fake, but the nipples are real. I can feel everything." Eva was talking to herself. The newfound sensitivity must have been hard for her to believe. "I can feel everything."

As she leaned her orbs closer to my face, Eva bore down on me and began her rhythm. Her years of experience were clear. She also knew the exact words to say to bring me over the finish line.

"Trust the universe, David. You are a good man. If it's meant to be, it will be. Don't stop loving her, ever. Now get back that confidence that has helped so many of us find our way. You broke through my barriers, sweetheart, showing me they were self-created. Now break through your own. Come to me. You are safe. I truly desire you. That hasn't happened in a long, long time. Fill me up. Affirm me by letting go. Let go, David. Trust and let go."

Her stiff pearl rubbed against me. Her strong inner muscles clinched me. But it was the authenticity in her eyes that took me there. I wasn't just another customer. I was her "client," a man she truly wanted to help. Eva was transforming before my eyes.

My self-control was returning, my confidence building. We worked as a team, two professionals at the top of their games, having world-class sex for the pure joy of the act.

Eva's face told me she could see the changes happening. Satisfaction morphed into glee. She giggled. It was as if we were two college students, fucking for fun on a dorm room carpet. I found it appealing to watch the years roll back for both of us.

Eva was jubilant. "Come on, big boy. Show me what you've got."

My hands clasped her hips, and she could see my biceps heave as I helped deepen her grind.

Her eyes widened as she realized that she was about to orgasm for the third time. She shook her head in recognition. "Three in a row, David. Three in a row. Come with me, baby. Come there with me now!"

She stiffened as she said, "Now!"

And we both let go.

The power of her inner grasp contracted as we both came. Waves of ecstasy washed over us. Sweat dripped off our bodies like two wrestlers at the end of a long, hard-fought match.

Eva bent down, her mouth locking with my own in one of the most gentle, tender kisses I could remember.

"Most men want me to suck their tongues out," she whispered. "I like this much better."

I caressed her cheeks with my fingers. We continued to kiss. We were middle school sweethearts, exploring the nuances of passion for the first time.

I imagined the thoughts going through our minds were probably very different, but in many ways, very much the same. I was reassessing my reality and contemplating my priorities. I considered what I might do when my singular profession no longer brought me fulfillment. And I was allowing myself to grapple with what life might be like without Ellen at its center.

When, at long last, I softened inside of her, Eva smiled.

"Well done, David," she said. "Well done."

"Trust the universe," I told her. "I will, if you will, Eva."

"It's Cecilia. Cecilia Gómez. That's my actual name."

"You are pretty fucking awesome, Cecilia Gómez."

"My friends used to call me CeCe."

Her voice sounded like a young girl, the person I imagined she used to be before life and the decisions she'd made had hardened her heart.

"Trust the universe," she repeated. "What a concept."

CeCe put her head on my chest, and we held one another, contemplating the challenges and the rewards that might be ours if we could find the courage to do just that.

20

TRUSTING THE UNIVERSE

DAVID
Men are more self-repressive than women. We push things down into our subconscious until the thing gets so full that it overflows and we crash and burn.

That was a stereotype. But it was my experience. And when things boiled over, damn did they boil over.

It was after three in the morning when I stumbled back to my condo. Monica would say that CeCe had blown my chakras wide open. Ellen would say that it was a cathartic experience I desperately needed. I thought CeCe was just amazed that there was still some authentic passion in her heart. I hoped she began dreaming about what life might be like in another trade.

I knew I was.

At six, I gave up trying to sleep and pulled up the calendar app on my phone. Ellen was due to get on a plane for London later in the day. For the first time, she was taking Elise with her. I imagined that her new love interest would assess Ellen's little sunshine, perhaps gauging whether he wanted a girlfriend with kid baggage.

At seven, I sent her a text.

Travel safe today, you two! I hope this guy is everything you've dreamed of. Always here for you in every season.

I must have reworked the wording a half-dozen times before I sent it.

Forty-five minutes later, Ellen sent me back a heart emoji and a picture of Elise blowing me a kiss. I figured she was just waking up.

At eight sharp, a text arrived from Mandy. **"Lunch today? Work-related."**

I shot her an affirmative. Instantly got an address back from her.

I had a long voice mail from Patricia, apologizing for ditching me last night and saying how little afterglow there was at her afterglow event. She ended it with, **"Next week, same time, same place."**

I knew Adrian got to the office at nine. I left a message with her admin, asking for an appointment to review my financial health. Adrian texted me a few minutes later.

Be here at 10.

At 10:02, I sat across from her in the now-familiar leather chair with the view of the city.

"Did you know that Ellen is building her dream house in Denver?"

I did not. "Colorado has always been her dream location."

"It's a subconscious sign for you to intervene in this Damon thing."

Adrian always thought things were subconscious signs.

I tried to change the subject.

"How is your love life?"

Adrian blushed. "Why do you always deflect when I talk about you and Ellen, David?"

I was looking for a life preserver. "How is Lance?"

"He failed the 'extra mile' test. I'm now on boyfriend number three. He's okay, but they all have the same problem."

I was prepared for a deep conversation about addiction, work-life priorities, or ex-wives. Adrian surprised me.

"None of them can keep up with me sexually. I'm just getting warmed up, and they burn out."

That was becoming an issue for Mandy. In the months since she became a regular, two things had happened. She was suddenly being invited to contribute to strategy meetings held by the top executives in her company. They had recognized her skills with a promotion to Project Manager. Mandy had entered the inner circle of the C-Suite. Her ideas were good, and her bosses were smart enough to listen.

The other development concerned her libido. She had two other men on the hook who not only found her attractive but were aggressively pursuing her because of her specific and spectacular skills.

Perhaps she and Adrian had more in common than I realized.

"Stamina requires conditioning," I said. "Give them a gym membership."

"Are you sure you wouldn't consider dropping your work-sex prohibition, just for an old friend?"

On that day, I thought about doing that.

"Maybe there's another way," I said. "How much money do I need if I want to retire?"

"Retire from the job you have? I thought you'd want to ride that pony as long as your back and your Cialis prescription would let you."

I wondered how much of what I said would get back to Ellen.

"Just pondering about my options," I replied, feeling like a coward.

Adrian wasn't buying my act. "I know what's happening. Ellen's got a boyfriend, and it's made you realize how hopelessly in love with her you are."

I tried to look surprised.

Adrian shook her head.

"Come on, David. Who knows the female species better than you do? The paradox here is that you have slept with more women during a committed relationship than any man on the planet. But, no man has ever been more faithful. Yeah, I have my own issues in the love department, but I'm not blind. The age difference means nothing, David. In your heart, you are married to Ellen. The one thing you two don't have is a license."

That was the reality I was afraid to face. It occurred to me that every relationship before Ellen had ended in abandonment. Had I built codependency with suffering? Was I setting myself up to lose her on purpose? I tried to shake these dark thoughts out of my mind.

"If that's the case, then explain why I have the career I have and why Ellen would entertain another option?"

"You have a unique gift. You don't control the women you meet. You help them find their mojo and free them from repressing healthy sexuality in a supportive, empowering, and," Adrian let out a long breath, "totally fulfilling way. Yes, I know some moralists would argue that last point, but it's the truth. The world is better because of what you do, my friend. I'm living proof. Ellen is just wrestling with her own shit. Yeah, there's some risk that she'll do something stupid and maybe even marry somebody to learn her lesson the hard way. But you two were born for one another. You are just starting to figure that out. Maybe she needs some time to come to the same conclusion."

"Have you and Ellen discussed this?"

"No. And I won't unless she asks me like you just did."

"I didn't ask you anything."

"I knew what you wanted to know the minute you walked in the door. So just admit that it scares you shitless so I can tell you what to do."

Always the left brain, I thought. That was my Adrian. "So, what should I do?"

"Have faith. Don't stop doing the things you do every day that show her how much you care. Support her own testing of the waters. You've been doing it for years without realizing it. Give her some space to do it, too."

"I'm afraid, Adrian. I'm afraid I'll lose her."

"She knows who you are. She counts on it. If you want to stop transforming our lives and enjoying the coital benefits that come with it, that's your call. But I bet there's a dual payoff every time someone else melts into your arms. You change a life and your dedication to Ellen becomes stronger."

Adrian nailed it. I found a productive way to enjoy intimacy without commitment. If I were ever going to get past grieving my parents, I would have to face this. I can't let go of the past without finding something to hold on to in the present.

I must have telegraphed my thoughts. Adrian nodded as she watched me process everything.

"Stay the course. Trust the universe."

There it was again. Trust the universe. I decided it was a sign.

"So, how much money do I have?"

Adrian didn't budge from the leather chair.

"More than enough. You could never earn another penny and live a life of luxury off of four percent of your portfolio value."

"How did that happen? I know what I started out with. It hasn't been that long."

"Thank Ellen. I got you into the Corbin Cosmetics IPO. The few who could buy shares at the strike price have already made a killing. Normally, I'd tell you to leave your cash there and watch it grow, but I've already diversified your profits. You own your car and your condo free and clear. You have no debt. And for a guy who seems to spend so much time traveling and having fun, your lifestyle is very frugal."

There was more.

"And guess what those years of financial education bought you? I made some investments based on your own research that have skyrocketed. Sandia would hire you as a senior analyst tomorrow just for your brains. Your annual performance bonuses alone will net you more than you earn in the bedroom in three years. You have plenty of options, my friend. Be patient, keep the faith, and stay the course. That's my advice if you want it."

The memory of my threesome with Adrian and Ellen that I thought I had lost in my alcohol haze chose that moment to manifest. Adrian had grown since that encounter. Ellen had, too. Was I the only one still stuck?

"You really are amazing, Adrian. And of my portfolio of bedroom partners, I have to say that you remain one of the best I've ever enjoyed."

Adrian shivered. "Nothing has come close to you since." There was the look. "What I wouldn't give for some more laps around lover's lane."

I relaxed enough to laugh. "I'm surprised you haven't taken advantage of a vulnerable man."

"Watch out, hot stuff. I know where you live."

"And in my current mental state, I would probably make an exception to my policy if you showed up."

I stood and walked to the door, hoping she didn't see what was happening below my belt.

"Hey," she said.

I turned. She put a thumb on the neckline of the white silk blouse beneath her blazer, dragging it downward to reveal her extraordinary cleavage. With her free hand, she pointed to my pants.

"I saw."

⚘

MANDY WAS NO LONGER THE RESERVED URCHIN I HAD FIRST MET. She had upgraded her wardrobe to match the crowd she now ran with. A lady's Rolex watch adorned her right wrist, and a string of pearls hung around her neck.

"Damn, woman. I am so proud of you!"

"Don't even think I called you here to fire you, David. We're on for Tuesday nights just like always."

"I wouldn't blame you for moving onward and upward, Mandy. You're out of my league."

Mandy blushed. It was a humble, attractive blush. I noticed something else that had eluded me during our weekly exercises. She had lost weight. I could see definition in the muscles that lay beneath her insulation. Her thinner face and those expressive eyes radiated the air of an executive.

"Not hardly," she said. "I need your help with something else. I want to figure out how to get to Robert Haden, and I don't feel like it's a strategic advantage to use my friendship with Monica to do it."

I was interested. "What's up?"

"One of our subsidiaries is about to spin up an enormous project in Asia. It's ideal for the Haden Corporation, but there are other competitors, and I want his help with the pitch. I know it will make my company a ton of money, and it has the potential to triple Haden's already substantial cash flow."

I had not talked with Robert Haden since our brief interaction in Florida. But I wouldn't bet against Mandy.

"I'll make the call. When would you like to see him?"

"ASAP. The deal is so complicated that it will take months to close. My company has deadlines that require starting serious negotiations now. And please, David, keep this conversation between us. When this thing goes public, whoever we associate with it, will get a huge bump in their net worth."

I thought about my investment position in Haden Corporation. It was significant.

"Done," I said, not knowing if I could even open a door. "Stand by your cell phone."

Mandy got up from the table and bent over to kiss me on the cheek.

"I wish there were more time to visit, but I have some more homework to do in case we get a meeting. Thank you, David. And —" Mandy ran her tongue across the bottom of her front teeth "— I'll taste you on Tuesday."

❧

Dear Mr. Haden,

I have always wanted to find some small way to thank you for your overwhelming generosity, not just to me but to so many others who are the beneficiaries of Haden Corporation's philanthropy.

My friend, Mandy Stillwell, has an interesting idea that might lead to a mutually beneficial opportunity. I've included her business card and cell phone in the event that you have some time to explore it.

She tells me that there is a bit of a short fuse, so if it's possible to see her this week, it will facilitate her ability to make things happen quickly in the event of your interest.

Warmest regards,

David Orion

෧෯෧

I DELIVERED THE HANDWRITTEN NOTE TO ROBERT HADEN'S secretary, who assured me she would give it to him immediately.

By the time I left the Haden building, it was nearing five o'clock. I felt suddenly exhausted and pointed my vehicle toward home. Work was a welcome distraction, and the knowledge that I was in a good financial position felt great. It was a rare night where I had no clients. I was eager to fill the jacuzzi and drink an ice-cold Coke.

In reality, I had made very little progress. The demons of my past still haunted me. I had created a career that had become tension relieving and not goal achieving. And the love of my life was slowly slipping from my grasp.

Day one of "trusting the universe" was in the books.

21

WITH DAMON WITH ELISE

ELLEN

The dimpled smile was waiting for us at customs and immigration. Damon squatted down to meet my daughter on her level.

"So this is Princess Elise," he said. "You look stunning, m'lady." Damon produced a stuffed animal from behind his back. "May I present Paddington Bear? As an official British icon, he and I want to welcome you to London."

Elise gave the animal a careful inspection, looking to me for permission to accept the gift.

"What do we say to Sir Damon, princess?"

Elise dipped her head, looking over the top of a pair of imaginary glasses at this handsome man with a strange accent. I was sold. She was still suspicious.

"Thank you very much," she squeaked.

Damon snaked an arm around my waist, waving to conjure up a chauffeur to push our luggage cart toward the exits.

"England has missed you," he said, tickling my earlobe with his nose. "And so have I."

꧁꧂

Damon's estate was about an hour's drive north of the city. It was a sprawling place, handed down from lord to lord until the family fell into poverty after World War II. Such were Damon's accomplishments that he could acquire it, fill it with servants, and rarely set foot on the grounds.

"I don't know why I keep the place," he sighed as he showed us around. "My life is a series of hotels and transactions. The thrill of the chase. The art of closing the sale. I feel blocked when I'm out here, too far from the action and helpless to influence things."

Damon rubbed Elise's head with a palm. "But, if I'm going to convince you to move to England, there must be change. How would you and Elise like to use this as your home base while you are here?"

It was my turn to explore an earlobe. "Only if you come with it."

"Of course, beloved." Damon's voice felt like velvet and satin. "I do have two evenings this week where I must focus on other clients. But I promise you, when we are together, you and the princess will get one hundred percent of my attention."

That sounded like something David would say. But there was a difference. David was always within reach. There were other clients in his life, too. And yet, I always knew we were his priority. Our lives revolved around the team. Could I convince Damon that my defini-tion of teamwork was a life worth living?

"I know where you're taking this, Damon," I said. "If we are going to consider cementing a partnership, I need to know that you will be an engaged dad and a faithful husband."

Damon closed his eyes, inhaling the sweet smells of the flower beds. "A family is the one thing I always wanted. My own parents divorced. They sent me to boarding school as soon as one would take me. So I have a lot to learn about being a father."

"Are you coachable?" I asked. "By the time we get to be our age, our habits are pretty much engrained."

"Coach me," Damon said. "I'm a man who is falling in love. The thought of living without you is much more painful than the chal-lenge of changing."

My knight guided us back toward the main house. Another wave and another woman appeared with her own three-year-old in tow.

"Ms. Ellen Corbin, meet Constance and Chloe. Constance is a neighbor, and I thought perhaps she and her daughter might give Elise a brief tour of the town, including a stop at our local ice cream emporium."

"Would you like that, baby?" I asked.

Elise shrugged. She knew the subtext of the offer as well as I did. Get the kid out of here so the adults can play grownup games. She kissed me and trotted off toward Constance and Chloe.

"A dutiful little girl," Damon observed. "Imagine what a British education and a few helpful connections could mean for her future."

"Is there ever a time when you are *not* plotting something?" I asked, exasperation creeping into my voice.

Damon swept me into his arms. My legs locked around his waist. I could tell that our next port of call would be the bedroom.

My knight winked at me.

"I'm always plotting something."

D
AVID
Most of the work associated with my singular profession took place at night. During the day, I absorbed the world of analytics.

I paid close attention to Tom Stafford's teachings, adding a few of my own insights into the analysis of the numeric ebb and flow that affects stock valuations. Together, we created a tool that became a key evaluation instrument for the company.

Without a clear view of my future, I had accepted a full-time gig with Sandia after earning my MBA.

Tom became one of my best male friends, the older brother I never had. He was one of the few in whom I confided my conflicting emotions about Ellen.

"The numbers say that relationships where the woman is older are three times more likely to fail," Tom said over an Arnold Palmer cocktail one lunch hour. "But there is no solid research behind why."

I sipped my Coke, trying to remove a piece of salad from between my teeth. "It has to be cultural. Society seems more willing to accept May-December romance where the guy is older."

"But you two are hardly May-December. Ellen has ten years on you. But you began your thing early enough in life where you were both still growing. That it's lasted this long tells me you could go the distance."

I wasn't so sure. "We're always encouraging one another to go out and find someone closer in age. She's dated a bunch of men, but most seem to be more interested in her money than in her heart. I think it's just a matter of time."

"And you? How many women your age have you actually 'dated?'"

Not a one. My night work was always with older women. And I rationalized that I was so busy that there was never any time to even explore the field.

Like an excellent attorney, Tom knew most of the answers before he asked the questions.

"You owe it to yourself and to Ellen to prioritize some exploration, my friend. You are making a ton of money now. You can afford to carve out one night a week for that project."

Ellen agreed. "You are definitely a Unicorn," she said, "Every girl's dream. Cast your net. Find someone who lights your fire." She ran her tongue across her upper lip. "Like you light mine. Find her.. and please her."

☙❧

TOM SAW THE ANNOUNCEMENT OF THE LOCAL SOFTWARE developers' club's monthly meeting and strongly suggested that I attend.

It turned out that she didn't want to be there, either.

It felt like a replay of how I had met CeCe. Two fish out of water, standing at the back of a room full of geeks, waiting for a chance to make a clean getaway.

I buried my head in my cell phone, studying some SEC data for an institutional investor. If it weren't for her initiative, I would have totally missed her.

"You're not enjoying this, are you?"

Her voice had a smart-aleck edge.

"Not really," I said, my gaze still focused on the screen.

"So, why are we here?"

The question got me to focus on her.

She could have been Ellen's younger sister. The same blond hair spilled over her shoulders, hers topped by a baseball cap with her company's logo on it. She had the body of a softball player, athletic and well-toned. A royal-blue fleece covered a black V-neck tank top. Jeans and running shoes completed the ensemble. A pair of reading glasses hung from the base of the V-neck. Her posture minimized the effect of what I decided must be a spectacular balcony.

Her makeup was minimal, enough to accent high cheekbones and dark eyebrows that made me wonder about her hair color's authenticity. Her lips pursed in a half-smile that didn't give me a sense of their depth.

But, just like Ellen, her deep-blue eyes reeled me in. They flickered in the tiny motions that telegraphed complete focus.

She was so stunning I forgot her question. She must have been used to the effect she had on men. Without prompting, she repeated it.

"So, why are we here?"

I regained my composure. "I'm sorry. Your question was exactly what was on my mind. When I start to focus on my screens, it's time to escape."

"Escape. I like that idea. You look like the only normal person here. Want to grab some coffee or something and tell me why?"

It was one of the better pickup lines I could remember.

"I'd rather be anywhere but here. Tell me your preference. As long as they have Coca-Cola, I'm in."

"Coke rots your teeth."

I grinned so she could see my perfectly aligned pearly whites. "Not yet, at least. I don't know what I'd do without the caffeine."

"Touché, Mr. Wonderful. There's a place a block down that has both your poison and mine. Follow me."

She held up a fist. I bumped it.

"I'm Amy. Amy King."

When we got to the coffee shop, I told my Sandia story, not yet ready to share the rest. I was much more interested in Amy King.

As one of the few left brains with a right brain, she was a senior project manager at a software firm. Amy possessed the magical ability to translate the binary brains of software engineers into colorful pictures that upper management could turn into cash. An MBA like me, augmented by an undergrad in computer science, Amy was rising quickly through the ranks.

She sipped what smelled like the strongest cappuccino on the menu. "Sounds like we are two peas in a pod."

I qualified it, "If you mean no work-life balance, we are."

"David Orion," she said. "That's vaguely familiar. How would I know you?"

My circulation was wide enough now. I worried that there might be a connection to the other dimension of my life. Why was I nervous about coming clean to her?

"I was at the U about the same time you were. Perhaps we knew some of the same people."

She was smarter than I realized. An uncomfortable chill ran down my back as I saw her putting the puzzle pieces together. In front of Amy, my carnal profession embarrassed me. How would she react when she figured things out?

"David Orion. They call you 'The Love Whisperer.'"

For the first time, being recognized made me blush. I couldn't understand why.

"Kimberly at Chakra's was a little too loose with some information when she was beating me up on the massage table a few weeks back. We talked about the dearth of decent males on the planet, and she said something like, 'I wish I were your age. I'd be all over David Orion like a bitch in heat.'"

"Kimberly exaggerates."

"Not from where I sit. If anything, she exaggerates the negative. She told me about your date night at the hospital. Well played, David. Well played. How old do you think I am?"

I learned to shoot low with older women. This was unfamiliar territory. The best I could do was to cough up mine.

"I'm twenty-six."

"Me too. And you are one of the youngest hotshots at Sandia

Wealth Advisers. Kimberly added that little postscript when she stopped drooling. 'He's rich, he's handsome, and he makes you come like an earthquake.' That was her conservative assessment."

"Now you're embarrassing me."

"Tell me something, David Orion. We've been talking for almost an hour, and you haven't hit on me once. You obviously do very well with the more seasoned among my gender. What am I? Cold pizza?"

"You're not cold pizza. In fact, you remind me of what I like most about my closest female friend. At least that's my first impression. And yes, I have a lot of sex, but I am rarely the one who initiates it. Sometimes I wish that my clients were more interested in conversation and less interested in gymnastics."

"You mean fucking."

"That's a synonym."

"Then use it. It's not like you are talking to a virgin."

I liked this girl. She had spunk.

"Okay. To be direct, women pay me to help them recover their mojo. In many cases, that involves fucking. I'm good at it. Not just the ins and outs. Women fascinate me. I want to understand the nuances of what empowers them and do my best to provide for them."

I took a pull off of my Coca-Cola.

"But I don't go chasing it," I said, feeling the buzz that the combination of sugar and caffeine always delivered. "You appreciate someone who stimulates your mind and not just your... cock."

Amy chuckled. "I know the feeling. And you're getting better. You flipped through three or four euphemisms before calling a cock what it is. That's progress."

Amy King leaned back, her shoulders relaxing against the wooden edge of the chair. I got the first sense of the extent of her endowments.

"Yeah, I figured that's where your eyes would go if I did that."

"You share another skill with my friend," I said, marveling at the similarities between Amy and Ellen. "You can read my mind."

"It's not mind reading. I kinda pushed them out at you, just to make sure you were normal. All my life, I've fended off males who like my body and couldn't care less about my brain. And the guys I work with are such nerd birds that I could walk into the bullpen topless and there wouldn't be a single boner among them. I just wanted to make sure you weren't like that."

"Oh, I appreciate abundance. But an interesting heart and mind are much more of a turn-on."

"Everybody says that. Few mean it."

I decided that I wanted to get to know Amy King. Slowly, and in our own time.

"Try me. My friends are challenging me to find a girlfriend who is closer to my age. I don't know if I even want one. If Kimberly is selling me to you, it's probably because you are looking for someone who loves your brain more than your boobs. The only way we'll know if we fit is to get better acquainted. Are you interested?"

A smile dawned across her face like a sunrise. "That is the most unromantic 'let's go steady' invitation I've ever had."

"So, how about it? The one ground rule will be that either of us can walk if we feel like it."

Amy King shook my hand. "Fair enough, David Orion. You may just be my kind of crazy. Let's find out."

⚜

ELLEN WAS ELATED. KIMBERLY WAS ECSTATIC. TOM WAS PLEASED that I took his advice. Adrian was suspicious.

"Chasing someone who looks and acts just like Ellen? Sounds to me like a fool's errand."

"Come on, Adrian. I finally do what everybody has been telling me to do and you give me shit about it?"

"You know who you really love. I wouldn't trust this Damon guy with a ten-pound note, let alone my best friend. Screw the age difference. Tell Ellen that the two of you were meant to be soul mates. Quit screwing around and make it official."

"I'll come to my own conclusions, just like Ellen will. Let me explore, will ya?"

"Mark my words. You're just wasting time. And you're going to break that girl's heart."

"I appreciate the vote of confidence."

"Listen, buster. If I weren't certain that you and Ellen were born for one another, I'd have you velcroed to my fat thighs with a ring on your finger, calling myself Mrs. Adrian Orion. Of course, Amy is going to fall for you. But can you fall for her when your heart already belongs to someone else?"

I would have to find that out in my own way, in my own time.

⚜

EVERY THURSDAY, FOR THE NEXT SIX MONTHS, I WAS WITH AMY. The more time we spent together, the more we liked one another.

Assets complimented weaknesses. We shared a common generational life experience. Although she came from a "normal" family, her sarcasm and cynicism were antidotes to my stoic outlook. Her intellect challenged me in a way that few of my clients ever did. She could be tender when I was down and kick my ass when I flew too high.

Amy told me that the attraction was my kindness and sense that I truly cared about others. "Most guys our age are still in the "me, me, me" stage of life. You would give everything to some nonprofit if it touched the right place in that big heart."

Without the trepidation of rejection, we talked candidly about our lives, loves, and fears. Both of us had been drawn to someone we thought was unattainable. We both were still uncertain about our future and our life's purpose. And Amy was surprisingly nonjudgmental about my evening activities. I felt safe with Amy, and she felt safe with me. We admired one another's strengths yet gave the other person permission to call bullshit when necessary.

As Ellen's relationship with Damon encroached on our weekends together, I began spending mine with Amy. We slept in the same bed. We kissed like I imagined married people did, sentimental pecks followed by long, meaningful hugs.

But we didn't have sex.

Ellen thought this was crazy. "You two are young and at the peak of your powers. Why aren't you fucking one another's lights out?"

"She's got the body," I admitted. "I want to learn about the mind that will sustain the relationship when our bodies can't."

It was a pretty good answer, masking the actual truth. I was already in love with someone else.

I would soon find out that Amy had Ellen's question on her mind, too.

My day job at Sandia was going so well that I won a trip to Hawaii. Since it was my foster dad's birthplace before he immigrated to the mainland, I offered the experience to Elliot and Kimberly. They had just announced their engagement, and I thought it would be a perfect way for her to meet his family.

Kimberly read me the riot act.

"There is no way we'll accept, David. Take Amy with you, find her G-spot, and ride the wild surf until you are both screaming for mercy."

I used the hotel money to book a romantic Airbnb on Maui, flew us, first-class, to Oahu, and rented a chopper to take us to our mountain paradise.

Amy bought an island wardrobe, and I did my best to look like Tom Selleck.

Our bungalow had a breathtaking view of the ocean, an outdoor shower, and no neighbors for almost a mile in all directions.

It was the perfect place to see if we were as compatible in bed as we seemed to be in every other dimension of our relationship.

The night we arrived, we cooked dinner together, a habit that grew out of Amy's love of the culinary arts. I even dispensed with my no-alcohol policy to share a bottle of wine with her as we sat in a porch swing on the lanai, watching a spectacular sunset.

"Are you happy, Ames?"

She put her head on my shoulder and nodded. "It's been an amazing six months."

She was warm and smelled wonderful. A gentle breeze had her in its sway. Her hair danced alluringly across her shoulders. If ever there were a younger version of Ellen, Amy was it.

"Have I convinced you I admire your heart more than your body?"

"Yeah. You've over-delivered on that one, Mister Wonderful."

Amy's eyes were undressing me. I scanned the flowery sundress cut to maximize her curves, the way her legs crossed, and how her toes wiggled playfully. She bit her lower lip as her eyes searched my own. She was firing every weapon in her arsenal to get my attention.

"You've treated me like a lady, like an equal, and like a best friend. You've done everything right, David. You have my permission to make love to me."

Her kisses began like many that came before a gentle peck. But she came back again and again, parting my lips and working on my mouth with increasing desire.

"Take me to bed, David Orion. Let's see if we are as compatible inside one another as we are on the outside."

I chuckled as I lifted her into my arms. "Now, who is using the synonyms?"

"Okay, big stuff, be prepared because I'm going to fuck you like you've never been fucked before. Is that more like what you'd expect me to say?"

There were no windows in our bedroom, just rectangles cut into the walls that allowed the breeze to caress us. I opened a skylight in the thatched roof to let the stars shine in.

We stood on opposite sides of the bed and began the mating ritual of undressing for one another.

I was still a weight-room devotee. I could see her reaction to my nakedness. "The look" was definitely in her eyes.

She slowly removed her sundress, revealing every nuance of her splendid figure.

My desire was rising. This was a longing, Ellen transmogrified into my generation, my own time and place, before the pain of divorce and the responsibility of a child, before becoming a CEO, before Damon.

Amy crawled onto the bed on all fours, her sumptuous bosoms swaying with each movement. She glued her eyes to my ever-increasing interest as it rose in tribute to her allure.

She gave it a single long lick, from bottom to top, pleased by its responsiveness.

Amy rose to her knees and applied my requisite condom. She put her arms around my neck. As I straightened, she wrapped her legs over my forearms so I could guide myself toward the wet warmth that awaited.

Now she focused on my mouth with more force, rocking her head to ensure that it left no corner without exploration.

I lifted her up and down to facilitate her moisture with my own still-thickening contribution.

I turned and sat on the bed, gliding down onto my back to give her control. At first, she continued to hold me close. The pace of her breathing quickened.

Then she slowly sat upright on top of me, her thumbs circling her nipples as her powerful legs directed me deeper and deeper into her.

I put my hands behind my head and marveled at the scene playing out before me. Amy was one of the most attractive, amazing women I had ever met. Our careful courtship had progressed through acquaintance, friendship, and to the brink of love. We understood our imperfections and respected one another in ways that many couples never did. And now, I learned that Amy had a sensuous side. She knew what she liked and had the skills and experience to get it. She also had known enough men to develop a telepathic feel for what I enjoyed and was delivering it to near perfection.

"Let yourself go, Amy," I prodded. "Show me what you're like when you lose control."

She seemed to exist in another time and place. Amy made love to me with a vengeance. I watched in awe as she worked with deliberation and will to bring herself to climax, taking in a huge breath and exhaling it in exaltation as she came.

Sweat shimmered on her body as she looked down at me. "Okay, Mister Wonderful. It's your turn. Show me how it feels to fuck her."

"What?"

"Pretend that I'm Ellen. Fuck me like you'd fuck her. I've talked to Kimberly. I know exactly what to do. Show me what it's like to give your all to your true love."

I was dumbstruck. What was happening?

"It's okay, David. I'll explain later. Give me this gift. Please. Love me as if I were her. I want to know.

I totally understand. Let this round be all about you. Take me as if I were her. I am Ellen Corbin, David. Fuck me now!"

Disarmed by Amy's revelation, all the pent-up emotions I had been suppressing came to the surface. I rolled her onto her back and started my cadence, tenderly touching her face, kissing her neck in the spot I knew Ellen loved. I massaged her nipples with my thumb and index finger, circling her pearl with the reflexive touch that drove Ellen wild.

Amy leaned back against the pillow, arching into every push. Her face seemed to radiate joy and happiness.

The more I thought about Ellen and Damon, the harder I pounded Amy. She groaned with each attack. Not a painful groan, but a guttural challenge for me to go deeper and pound even harder.

Her nails dug into my back as she worked with me. There was a dampness that I knew must be blood.

"Come on, David. More! More! Harder! Get it out. Give it to me!"

Finally, the alchemy of sensation, sound, and emotion brought me to the summit. I thrust deep inside of Amy and released. Her eyes glowed. She pulled my face toward hers. Amy's kisses did what she intended them to do.

She turned her attention to my ear, licking the earlobe and whispering, "Give me all of it, David. Every last drop. All of it."

Even though I still saw clients throughout our courtship, it felt as if I hadn't come in months. My sex with those who paid me did not even scratch the surface of the turmoil I felt in my heart.

I continued to produce until the condom inside Amy exploded. The added sensation and the gush of liquid was an experience we would both never forget.

"Again," she whispered. "Let me feel you without a barrier."

I knew that she had taken her own precautions. I pulled out just long enough to rip the shredded prophylactic off and returned to her. The sensations were incredible. I suddenly longed to be with Ellen in this same uninhibited way.

Amy's sixth sense detected my unspoken desire. She encouraged me.

"Over there. Take your Ellen over there."

She pointed to an overstuffed chair in the room's corner.

I picked her up without losing my penetration, and we moved together across the room. Amy brought her feet up onto the arms of the chair. It was the perfect height for me to kneel on the soft rug beneath it and touch the exact inner erogenous zones that were her favorites.

She guided my hips with increasing speed until she climaxed again, her moans slowly growing into a hedonistic scream that echoed into the Hawaiian night.

"Back to the bed, sweetheart. Let's lie side by side as one, as who we both really are."

Amy threw her arms around my neck and her legs around my back. I picked her up. She saw our reflection in a mirror that hung above the dresser.

"Wait."

We both stared at the sight. We were so soaked in sweat that it looked as if we had just come out of the shower.

"I want to make a memory," she whispered. "A memory of what might have been."

We lay side by side, Amy's legs interlaced with mine to facilitate the coital connection that made us one.

She held me tightly. Her words were caring and comforting.

"I know exactly how you feel, baby. I know. When I was riding you? It wasn't at all about us then. It was about him, my version of your Ellen. As I loved you, I was loving him. It was extraordinary, the best sex I've ever had. I understood long ago what this thing of ours was really about. We were testing ourselves. Could someone else fill the void? Tonight proved it. We can have great sex, and we can be great friends. But our hearts are owned by others. Thank you, David. Thank you for helping me prove that to myself. I hope I could help you illuminate your own truth. I now understand the depth of your feelings for Ellen. You deserve her. She needs you. Don't let her go."

At that moment, Amy and I moved into a relationship we could never have imagined.

Gratitude overwhelmed me. I wanted to thank her in the most intimate way I knew.

But first I had a question.

"Is he truly unattainable?"

Amy shrugged. "It sure feels like it. I've tried everything I know to help him see how much I love him. I know he doesn't have another person in his life. I'm missing something, and I wish I knew what it was."

Enlightenment dawned on me. "Ahh. Perhaps I can add some value, after all.

༄༅

THE REST OF THE WEEK FELT LIKE A PERVERSE HONEYMOON. HERE we were, two damaged souls who knew each other's hearts like few ever do. We cavorted in the ocean. We saw the sights. We ate sumptuous meals. And we had glorious sex every night. Deep conversation between two close friends, committed to helping one another find happiness, always followed the sex.

CeCe had opened me up to vulnerability, but it was Amy who gave me the gift of a smart listening ear, as someone who knew me well enough to help me, without the attachment that could blind her to what was in my best interest.

On our last night on the islands, we lay facing one another on the bed that was now as familiar to us as our own, making memories of one another's nude bodies. We knew that tonight would be the last time we would share such intimacy.

"Does this guy really know what he wants in a partner?" I asked.

"I think he's blind as a fucking bat. I need to help him see."

"Do you want him to be happy, even if it means it's with somebody other than you?"

"I don't know, David. I just don't know. In my best heart of hearts, I want that. But I can't help feeling like he's the soulmate who was born bonded to me."

"Then court him like you courted me. Keep enough emotional distance to decide if it truly is the right thing. Trust the universe, Amy. If it's meant to be, it will be. If it isn't, I know that there is someone out there for you."

I caressed her cheek with a finger.

"You taught me that sometimes it takes a two-by-four to the side of the head to help you understand what you really want."

"So, what will you do now, Mister Wonderful? Will you sweep Ellen off her feet and toss this Damon guy to the curb?"

"I'm afraid I must trust the universe, too, Ames. I need to keep being me. If it's right, it will happen. I need to believe that. It's just so hard to do it."

Amy King circled her tongue around my lips. "If the universe has other plans, I'll be glad to walk beside you as we both figure them out."

We came together in every sense that night. It would be as much a turning point in my life as was that first morning when a blonde in a bathrobe had opened her door and forever changed me.

23

NOBODY'S PERFECT

ELLEN
The view from Damon's master bedroom took my breath away. In the morning, tufts of fog skimmed the top of the tree-lined road that wound its way through the estate. The place stood on a hill that rolled gently downward to reveal rural England's panorama that had inspired James Herriot to write about animals and Shakespeare to write about love.

This whole thing with my knight felt like a dream. Construction of Corbin Cosmetics, UK, was well underway. Whenever a cloud appeared on the horizon, Damon could brush it aside.

On the flip side, his notorious romantic past was fodder for the tabloids. They already speculated that his "relationship with the American Fragrance Queen might finally lead to nuptials."

His nights away happened more often than I liked, and while he was attentive to Elise, Damon had yet to forge the relationship David had with her.

"Things are different over here," he told me. "Kids know we love them; we Brits just show it differently."

Damon showed it by enrolling Elise in dance class, signing her up for a soccer team, and hiring an array of tutors to ensure that her intellectual growth matched her physical development.

He spent the money but was less interested in spending the time. Elise became close with Constance and Chloe, mostly because Damon and I had so many work-related social events that my daughter was spending more time with the neighbors than she was with us.

"In no time, your princess will have her own interests," Damon assured me. "It's good to expose her to as many things as possible so she can develop."

"In other words, you can't wait until she's old enough not to want to be with us?" I asked.

"I look forward to the age where she can have conversations on our level," he answered.

A picture of David, down on all fours, speaking gibberish to an enthralled two-year-old, came back to me. Was Elise's childhood merely a phase, like David and I had been? Even if it was, I didn't want to hurry it.

❧

As the year came to a close, we were back at Le Gavroche. Business was booming. I was becoming richer by the day. I owed much of my international success to the man who sat across from me.

When the wine was decanted, Damon raised his glass. "To the woman who taught me the true definition of happiness."

"To Corbin Cosmetics, UK," I added, "and to everyone who helped make it real."

"To everyone," Damon allowed, swirling his glass before taking a long drink.

The wine was wonderful. The atmosphere in the restaurant was the ultimate in culinary romanticism.

I should have expected what happened next.

Damon shifted his right hand to reveal a tiny blue box. I knew what was inside.

"Dearest Ellen," he began, "in the brief time we have been together, you have truly transformed me. My life, so far, has been a good one. But I never dared to dream that I would find the one thing that was missing: someone to share it with."

Damon flipped open the box with a thumb, revealing a gargantuan diamond ring, surrounded by a clutch of red rubies. He slid off of his chair and onto a knee.

"That someone is you, Ellen. Will you do me the honor of becoming my wife so that our love story might never end?"

It was the perfect proposal, something I could never believe would have happened to me. A knight was actually on his knees, asking for my hand. The atmosphere intermingled with Damon's words to intoxicate me.

That was a moment where the calculus of romantic love should mix with sober deliberations about what might lead to future conflict. I worked a balance sheet in my head. Damon was far from perfect. Did his strengths outweigh his faults? No man was ideal. Was Damon close enough to what I wanted? What I needed?

A string quartet materialized behind me. The music further dulled my ability to concentrate.

Damon prodded me. "Will you marry me, Ellen?"

24

THE LAST DANCE?

ELLEN
 I didn't wear Damon's ring when I came back to the States. I wanted to tell David about it first. And I was excited to hear about his trip with Amy. Could it be that we both would find what we were looking for?

David came home from Hawaii a changed man. He seemed more reflective, less communicative, troubled?

He arrived at Elise's bedtime. Naturally, she wanted him to tuck her in. What caught my attention was the absence of the laughter that was part of their routine. A familiar melody drew me to the doorway. It was dark in the hallway. They couldn't see me watching.

My daughter had curled up in David's lap on the upholstered glider that had been her rocking chair since birth. Her legs hung over his thigh, and her head rested against his neck as his powerful arms encircled her.

I recognized the melody. John Denver's "Sunshine" was playing on Elise's smart speaker. David was singing to her. It came rushing back to me: a vivid memory of watching my girl sit in David's lap as a two-year-old, mesmerized by an ocean sunset. The visuals were different, but the soundtrack was the same.

Tonight I heard cracks in David's whispered melody. As my eyes adjusted to the dark, I realized they were both crying.

I couldn't understand why, but I felt a wave of sadness wash over me. The picture drifted out of focus as my own tears filled my eyes.

The David had been part of our lives replayed in my mind, emotion building with each recollection. Our first meeting on Spring Street, the fantastic threesome with Adrian, and the emotional highs and lows we shared were highlights. The small moments had more power. Walking by the ocean with Elise between us. Breakfasts in bed. Date nights at Mariano's. And the safety and peace I always felt drifting off to sleep in David's arms.

As the final chorus of "Sunshine" came around, I had to walk away. A sense of melancholy overwhelmed me. I didn't know why.

🙐🙖

I EXPECTED A DETAILED AND STEAMY DOWNLOAD OF HIS adventures with Amy. I was looking for validation that releasing David for Damon was the right thing to do.

All David said was, "She was wonderful. But we are on different paths."

"Come on, my love. There's more to the story, and I want to hear it."

We were in our usual places, on the far ends of my living room sofa. It was that time when we shared our most intimate thoughts.

David was silent, but I could feel his eyes searching mine. When he finally spoke, it was about me.

"Tell me how things are going with Damon."

I wasn't about to let David off the hook. But I decided he would tell me about Amy in his own time.

"I think he may be the one. He has so many of the qualities I admire in you. He is attentive to Elise. He challenges my mind. It feels like he genuinely loves me."

"How do you know when it's true love, Ellen?"

That was a question that I wondered if he were asking for my benefit or his own.

"I guess love is something that evolves. I had a different understanding of the word when I thought I loved Brad. You taught me that love goes way beyond passion. It's two people, looking forward in the same direction, maintaining their individuality but committed to a partnership that makes the pair stronger together than they might be alone."

"Is that how you feel about Damon?"

I thought so. Damon was as committed to the success of Corbin Cosmetics as I was. He had been successful on his own, so there didn't seem to be jealousy about my accomplishments. He had the drive to explore new things and a hunger for life that made him attractive. That felt like the total package. And that night at Le Gavroche? I had said, "yes."

Looking at David, I wasn't so sure. "I think I do."

David slowly nodded, as if he were coming to a decision.

He smiled at me. But it was a different smile. If I didn't know how much he wanted me to find my happiness, I would have interpreted it as sadness, resignation. I suddenly felt a distance between us I'd never experienced before.

But I decided not to trust my instincts. David was always my biggest supporter. Maybe he was just processing the fact that, for me, at least, our dreams were coming true.

"Then maybe it's time," he said.

"Time for what?"

David stood. He walked toward the stereo system that fed the speakers in the room, connecting his smartphone to it via Bluetooth. He touched the screen. In a moment, Michael Bublé's voice enveloped the room.

It was "Save The Last Dance for Me."

He held out his hand. "May I have the honor?"

I arose, melting into his arms as he began softly singing along.

Our movements didn't reflect the energy of the song. It was as if we were young lovers, holding one another close in someone's finished basement.

And the lyrics didn't fit the moment. This was supposed to be a celebration of a dream coming true.

I felt a strange sense of loss, almost as if a fundamental piece of me was dying.

Our movements slowed. By the time Michael finished, we were stock still, just holding one another.

Our embrace lingered, even as I felt like our bond was breaking.

When I finally looked into David's eyes, they were filled with tears. I realized mine were, too.

"No matter what you do. I will still love you," he whispered, his voice cracking.

"Come to bed with me," I said. It sounded like I was begging.

David shook his head and kissed me on the forehead.

"I need to go."

I didn't want him to. But somewhere in the deepest corner of my soul, I understood.

I took his face into my hands and kissed him. It was tender and loving and long. I realized I didn't want it to end.

And then he was gone.

25

MEETING DAMON'S EX

DAVID
 Ellen told me she was engaged on the anniversary of the day we met.

Damon had wooed her well. He spoiled Elise and treated Ellen like a queen.

I had to hand it to the guy. He knew how to close the deal.

But inside, it devastated me. The wedding was to take place in six months. Ellen asked me to be her best man. I chivalrously declined, suggesting Adrian was a more appropriate maid of honor. New life. New start. I would be there for her, but she was Damon's now.

We didn't see much of one another after the night I came home from Hawaii. She reached out several times, but I always managed to be busy. We limited our conversations to benign text messages in the middle of the night, London time. She was already spending most of her evenings at Damon's. I learned he was a peer, a member of the House of Lords with some minor title. Ellen would carry the female equivalent and become a British citizen after the nuptials.

Everything about this felt wrong. That wasn't the ideal life Ellen had so often described. My gut told me that a guy who had spent most of his adult life avoiding commitment would struggle to live up to her expectations, especially as a step-father to Elise. I knew now that part of my attachment to her was to make up for my own childhood cut short. And the passage of time had dimmed the age difference, just as Adrian had said it would. Her announcement stunned Ellen's local friends.

"It should have been you, David," was Kimberly's reaction.

"She's the center of your life force," Monica told me. "All the good things that you both are stem from that partnership."

"When are you going to do something about this?" Amy asked. "I know, better than anyone, about the depth of your commitment to this woman. Just tell her before she does something she'll regret."

When the invitation came to attend the engagement party, I booked a flight.

Damon Winslow, CBE, threw Ellen a spectacular event worthy of his position and her popularity. It was the first time I'd seen a magnificent English estate up close.

Imagine Highclere Castle in *Downton Abbey,* and you'll get the picture. A phalanx of servants brought unending trays of hors d'oeuvres. They took drink orders, instantly appearing with perfectly prepared cocktails. A live eighteen-piece band played on the veranda overlooking the vast moor, framed by rolling hills and thickets of lush trees.

Ellen's guests were in the minority, surrounded by the famous and near-famous from Damon's circle. The wardrobes were as diverse as the invitees, from black-tie formal to jeans and leather jackets.

Ellen played her part to perfection. I watched her easily interacting with the English Prime Minister. I thought again of how much she had grown since we had met.

Facing Damon in the long reception line, I felt uncomfortable and out of place.

The future groom was in character, grinning as he wrung my hand. "I'm honored to meet you, David. From what Ellen tells me, you have worked wonders in her life."

He was shorter than Ellen preferred, eye to eye with her and equally svelte, a product of the trainer's artistry, enhanced by the tailors at

Saville Row. His dirty blond hair was too perfect not to be a dye job. I wondered if Ellen had figured that one out. The skin on his face pulled rubber-band tight against his skull. I searched his hairline for the micro scars plastic surgeons try to hide after a facelift. I watched his gray eyes focus on a person in one moment and totally dismiss them the next.

I tried to be the essence of magnanimity. "It's been a two-way street. I'm the one who's been the beneficiary. She's the most spectacular woman I've ever met."

"On that," Damon said, "we are in total agreement. And I promise you this: I will spend the rest of my life making her the happiest woman on Earth."

With that, Damon Winslow turned his attention to the long line of well-wishers and the Minister of Parliament who was next.

I stepped forward to face his betrothed. Ellen looked incredible. She wore a long, flowing sleeveless dress, drenched in a flower pattern. A crown of white roses encircled her head. She stood next to her husband-to-be with Elise at her side. Ellen being Ellen, she knew exactly the proper form to greet the heads of state and royalty in attendance.

I took her hands in mine, kissing her on the cheek.

"You've come a long way from 3480 Spring Street."

"I wouldn't be here today without you, my love."

My love. It didn't feel like that was an appropriate term anymore. I wanted to blurt out, "Don't do this, Ellen. *Ours* is the true love of your life." But I didn't.

Elise was in the middle of stealing an hors d'oeuvre off a serving tray when she recognized me. She dropped the toothpick that stabbed her snack and jumped into my arms.

"Uncle D! Where can we go and play?"

"You are playing, chipmunk. It's a game called movie star."

Her eyes brightened. "How do we play movie star?"

"We pretend that every one of these people came to see you because you are a famous movie actress. And you curtsy to each of them and say your magic movie line."

"What is my magic movie line, Uncle D?"

"'It is an honor and a privilege to meet you.' And then you say 'sir' if the person is a man and 'ma'am' if they are a woman. Got it?"

"I got it."

I tried to put her back down next to her mother, but she tightened her grip around my neck.

"I'm afraid, Uncle D," she whispered. "Afraid I won't ever see you again when Mommy gets married."

She knew exactly what Ellen and I were avoiding.

I tickled her ear with my nose and whispered back, "I love you, chipmunk. Wherever I may be, know that my heart is always with you and your mom. Ready to play movie star?"

Elise nodded. She let me put her back next to Ellen.

"Elise," Ellen said, pointing to the guy who came after me in line. "This gentleman is a member of Parliament. He helps make the laws here in Great Britain."

"It is an honor and a privilege to meet you, sir," Elise said, executing a perfect curtsy. She looked at me and rolled her eyes. "Do I have to be this nice to everyone, Uncle D?" she mouthed.

"Only tonight, chipmunk. Be sure to tell Mom what you really think when she tucks you in."

I winked at Ellen. There was something in her expression that I had not seen in some time. I couldn't quite place it. But it troubled me. Perhaps we were both realizing that the "last dance" I always saved for her had finally come and gone.

Damon was kind enough to ensure that there was a Coke with my name on it. I found an empty corner and stood against the wall, taking in the scene.

A stunning redhead, who could have been Sarah Ferguson's double, appeared out of the maelstrom. She wore an evening dress that clung to her like a neoprene wetsuit. She sidled up beside me with a glass of champagne in hand.

It felt like she was salivating as she inspected me.

"So, you are the famous David Orion. The consort, a generation younger than the bride-to-be."

"Guilty as charged."

"The 'Love Whisperer' is what they call you here. 'The man who can seduce any woman.'"

"It's a generous exaggeration."

"That's not what Damon tells me."

I tried to change the subject. "How do you know Sir Damon?"

"Just another piece of wreckage in his wake. One of many past girlfriends who ultimately lost out to your Ellen."

I hoped that Damon had truly put her in his rear-view mirror. Although she had the physical goods, her vibe felt like a self-centered cougar, about to pounce.

"Well," I said, "he has good taste. You look stunning."

She held out a bent hand, in the tradition of English royalty. "Felicity. Felicity Mountbatten."

I kissed it, as was the expectation.

"Royal blood?"

"In name only. I was married to a distant cousin for a brief time. The name sounds much better than my maiden name: Huxley."

I made the connection. "*Brave New World*. That name isn't too shabby in literary circles."

She was suddenly cold as ice. "I don't circulate in literary circles, David."

My patience was wearing thin. "Too bad, Felicity. There is a lot to learn there."

"So, are you as good a shag as everyone says you are?"

To her, the game was on, but I had no intention of playing it.

"I'm even better. But I'm off duty. Tonight is about Ellen."

"All rich people have assignations, David. The most confident invite them to their engagement parties."

I felt myself getting angry.

"Is that why you're here? A final kindness to an ex-lover?"

"There are at least four of us. Damon can be insatiable."

She circled a pink tongue around her ruby red lips.

The menace in my voice surprised me. "That had better be in his past."

Felicity laughed. It was a fake laugh that made me want to slap the smile off of her face. "There are new chapters written every day, love." She leaned in to whisper into my ear, "How would you like to be one of mine?"

I knew that if I didn't bolt, I would say something regrettable.

"It's been illuminating to meet you, Felicity. I wish you well."

I bowed, abruptly leaving her standing there. I dove back into the crowd, feeling sick to my stomach.

There was a tug on my sleeve.

"How do you like the British?"

Adrian. Thank God.

"If they are all like the groom's ex, who I just met, I'll stay on our side of the ocean."

Ellen's financial adviser—and maid of honor—was working hard on getting drunk.

"There are so many fucking people here that I can't breathe. Want to escape and get some air?"

I did. Adrian and I meandered our way through the maze until we found a servant. He opened a twelve-foot oak door that led out to a porch on the opposite side of the house to where the band was playing. It was relatively quiet and deserted. Ornately carved wooden chairs, protected by thick pillows, were separated by small tables; the entire scene was illuminated by candlelight.

We selected a pair and sat as far from the action as possible.

Adrian had taught one of the bartenders to concoct a nutcracker. My teetotaling nose could decode its unique bouquet. The slur in her voice told me she'd consumed several.

"The duchess is making a mistake, you know," she said. "Most Brits I've met are good people. She's chosen poorly."

I chuckled. "Always the left-brain analyst, my sweet. If Damon is a cad, he's sure not acting the part. He's great with Elise and seems to treat Ellen like a queen."

"He does suck-up to her daughter. But it's an act. Anything to close the sale. Yes, Damon has had two successful startups, but he's blown most of the money. He sees Ellen as his next meal ticket."

I didn't want to believe it. "But you made sure she got an iron-clad prenup."

"There are many ways to drain a bank account, handsome. I don't trust that shit."

"I guess we have to trust Ellen. She's a smart woman in her own right."

Adrian dismissed this with a look of disgust. "There's an old Yiddish saying, David. 'When you get a boner, you bury your brains in the dirt.'"

I laughed out loud. "I'm sure that's not a literal translation."

"But you get the drift. Ellen sees an older version of you. Judging by the number of enhanced chests in the house, Damon has developed some pretty effective bedroom skills that he has likely practiced on her. I hope she can separate fact from infatuation."

"That's her call, Adrian. I won't do anything to influence it."

Adrian turned her gaze to the exquisite sky above us. She pointed at my constellation. Orion was overhead. His belt pointed straight at us. "Is that what someone who truly loved her would do?"

That one hit home. From that moment on, it haunted me day and night.

✥ 26 ✥

ADRIAN - PART 2

DAVID
The interval between Ellen's engagement party and her wedding day flew by.

Eighteen months had transpired since I had arranged a meeting between Mandy and Mr. Haden. She was mum about the outcome. I had assumed the deal had fallen apart.

I received a cryptic text message from Mandy. Her Haden deal was happening.

She closed it with, **"It wouldn't have happened without you, David."**

Patricia became engaged to John, so both CeCe and I had lost clients.

I flew down for the dedication of "The Haden Institute for Aquatic Medicine" and was happy to learn that Monica and Frank were an item. Robert Haden actually shook my hand. "Wisdom comes in all shapes and sizes," he said, clapping me on the back. "He who stops learning begins to die."

THE WEEK BEFORE ELLEN'S WEDDING, I QUIETLY CANCELED WITH all my scheduled clients and retreated to the condo to grieve. The one woman I truly loved was committing to another. My sense of honor wouldn't let me share her bed or her body ever again.

I broke my alcohol prohibition and was two glasses into the second bottle of Malbec when the doorbell rang.

Adrian stood there—in

jeans, a zippered fleece, and flip-flops, she looked like a teenager.

"Hey," she said, as she inspected my bare feet, sweatpants, ragged workout shirt, and half-empty wineglass. "I figured you could use some company tonight."

I held the door, beckoning her to enter. "I don't have any nutcrackers, so this red stuff will have to do," I said, offering up the wine bottle.

Adrian could see the damage I'd already done to the contents. She pulled a glass from the cupboard and filled it, chugging the contents before reloading and draining a second dose.

"I guess I have some catching up to do."

"You're Uber-ing home if you keep that up," I warned.

"I'm not going home. Where are you wallowing?"

Adrian spilled some of her wine as she swung the glass in a wide angle, looking for a place to park.

I pointed to the couch, the one piece of Monica's furniture that I had saved when I refitted the place to my taste. We plopped down next to each other, putting our legs onto the long glass table with the bonsai tree in the middle. We drank, watching the confluence of the city lights with the clear starlit evening.

"I've never forgotten that incredible threesome," she said, her voice beginning to slur. "Nobody since has equaled your shower performance."

We toasted it.

"And nobody can ever equal your skill as my financial adviser," I said, trying to keep her libido in check. "My net worth is north of four million as of this morning. Thank you."

We toasted again.

"How are things in the wide world of single men?"

She sniffed.

"Bloody awful. Now that I finally feel attractive, this small pond doesn't have a single fish that interests me. Thanks for setting such a high fucking standard."

I told her I was considering not attending the wedding. "Sir Damon probably isn't all that jazzed about having a past admirer in the house on his wedding day."

Adrian was nonplussed. "Fuck him. I've seen the guest list. There are a dozen of his past conquests on it. You should show up and screw every one of them just to piss him off."

I thought of Felicity, the redhead. The conversation was sobering me up when I wanted, only to feel numb.

"Bide your time," she said. "I give Ellen six months at most before she dumps him."

I was still grasping. "It's good for Elise. She'll go to the best schools. Damon says he wants to adopt her."

Adrian scowled at me. "Quit trying to find a silver lining. This is a four-alarm cluster fuck. It's wrong. The universe has screwed this one up royally."

"There's nothing left to do but accept it. I've always wanted Ellen to be happy. If this is how she defines it, then so be it. She has already influenced my life in so many ways. I will always honor her for that."

"That's absolute bullshit," Adrian barked. "Why have you done nothing to rescue this woman from a dreadful decision? You are totally and hopelessly in love. Why won't you fight for it?"

Adrian had trouble deciding which of the four glass tables her intoxicated eyes were seeing dance in front of them was real. She selected one from the prism and put her glass onto it.

"It's her life, Adrian. Ellen gets to decide what she wants."

"If she thinks Damon is what she wants, then she's more delusional than I imagined. You two have always prioritized honesty. If you were honest and I were Ellen, what would you tell me right now?"

Don't do it. I love you. I love Elise. We are supposed to be together forever. Those were among my thoughts. My words were different.

"I'd just tell you that, 'No matter what you do, I will still love you.'"

Adrian shook her head. "That fucking song again. What sort of shower do you have in this place? I feel like it's time to revive an old memory."

She unzipped the fleece. She was naked beneath it; her glorious breasts swung free before my eyes.

"I'm not wearing any underwear, either."

She was feeling the wine.

I wasn't in the mood. Everything felt wrong.

"Are you doing this out of pity?" I asked.

"No. I am doing it because I am horny, angry, and sad. You are about to lose the love of your life. My best friend is about to make a gargantuan mistake. You and I need to ease our discomfort with an all-night fuck-a-thon."

"I don't think I can do it, Adrian. You have never looked more delectable, and I've never desired you more. But I feel like someone is about to die and I'm waiting for a call from the hospital."

Adrian stood. She snagged one of my arms and slung my body over her shoulder. The ease with which she could do it surprised me.

"You're going to throw your back out," I warned.

She pointed to the bedroom. "Not in the living room. In there, maybe. We're gonna see about that right now."

Somehow, Adrian made it to my room and tossed me onto the bed. She stood at the edge, shedding her fleece and blue jeans. She tossed her flip-flops one at a time toward a chair near the window. She missed both shots.

Like Mandy, Adrian had honored her body by changing her fitness regimen. Between a personal trainer and a dietitian, she had sculpted her figure. She was stunning.

Adrian's slur disappeared. Her face radiated warmth and kindness.

"Look, David. You helped me see that my situation wasn't nearly as dire as I thought it was. At least let me try to return the favor. Try to put Ellen on the shelf, at least for tonight. Let's see what we have both learned about pleasing one another in the years since we first met."

Adrian stripped me bare in record time. She hovered over me, about to attack.

"Remember what I said about velcroing you to my fat thighs? You're about to find out what that feels like."

That's when my cell phone rang. I recognized the caller ID and grabbed it.

"Ellen?"

She was crying. "David? You're there. Jesus fucking Christ on a pogo stick. I caught Damon cheating on me."

I tried to calculate the time difference. Eight-thirty plus five hours made it one-thirty in the morning in London.

"Where are you, Ellen? What's happened?"

Adrian, suddenly stone-cold sober, slid next to me, sitting upright, legs crossed, motioning to put Ellen on speaker. I did. Ellen's words flowed amidst sobs and curses.

"I had a work thing tonight. I was supposed to be up in Brighton with the chief marketing officer for this retail chain. But the guy got food poisoning, so I took the jet back to Gatwick and surprised Damon. It was after midnight when I got to the estate. Goddamn him. I walked into the bedroom, and there he was, butt fucking this silicone Sarah Ferguson cosplay. She's apparently an ex-ex-girlfriend. The staff told me that the bastard has been banging her for the last two months behind my back! Holy shit. Elise was sleeping in the next room! He's fucking an old girlfriend the week before his wedding with his soon-to-be step-daughter in the next goddamn room!"

Adrian whispered, "Where is she now?"

"Ellen, Ellen—where are you?"

"I grabbed my sleeping kid and left. Walked out. Woke the limo driver and told him to take me to London. Damon came running after us saying, 'I can explain,' and I'm yelling at him, 'there's nothing to explain. If you're going to fuck her, you can't fuck me.'"

She came down from her hysteria long enough to mutter, "Which

I thought was a pretty memorable way to put it, considering how pissed off I was."

The sobs resumed.

"Dammit, David, I don't know what to do. It's like husband number one all over again, but this time I'm the goddamn prize, the crown fucking jewels. What's wrong with me, David? Why is this happening again? He seemed so right, so kind, so—so *you!*"

My heart skipped a beat.

Adrian was whispering, "Whatever you do, *don't* tell her I'm here! Do you get that? Don't tell her I'm here."

I did the exact opposite. "Adrian's here, baby. She's been listening to me wallow all evening. She's been so supportive of you and me. Are you at a hotel?"

"I keep a room at the Savoy in Covent Garden, in case I have something late in the city. Elise slept through the entire thing, the screaming, my dragging her out of bed, all of it. She's snoring on my bed."

"What's your advice, Adrian?" I asked. "What should Ellen do now?"

Adrian's mind was in top gear. "Does Damon know about the hotel?"

Ellen was silent for a moment. "Probably not. I haven't used it at all since we got together. And he doesn't have this cell number. Giving that to him was going to be one of my wedding presents. That fucker. He'll never get it now."

"Get out of town first thing in the morning, girlfriend. Take a carry-on and wear what you're wearing if you have to. I'll call the travel agent right now and get a confirmation. If I remember correctly, there's a 7:50 a.m. Emirates flight that will have you at JFK by early afternoon."

Adrian punctuated her message with one more piece of advice. "Get as far away from that son of a bitch as you can. I'll call your lawyers in the morning and make sure he regrets ever dropping his pants."

As I took Ellen off the speaker, Adrian turned to her cell phone and started dialing.

Ellen, the CEO, was recovering. "Adrian can have the jet meet me there and bring me home. Oh, God, David! What did I almost do? Can you meet me at JFK and fly back with Elise and me? My heart is a mess, and you're the only one—"

Ellen stopped cold.

There was a long silence. I was about to ask if she was still there when I heard her voice shaking as the sobs returned.

"You *are* the only one, David. How could I have been so blind to that? Jesus. What I almost did. David, promise me you'll be there. Elise has been asking about you every day. I miss you. I need you. I —" I heard her choking on her words— "I love you."

The words had a new meaning. They went well beyond her definition the day she had first said them to me in her big new house with her new financial security and the world as her oyster. The reality we had both worked so hard to avoid was now crystal clear. The ideal relationship we both tried to seek elsewhere had begun that morning on Spring Street. It had only deepened with the passing of the years. True love was staring us in the face, and we were both too blind to see it.

The calm confidence that I always seemed to find when Ellen needed it most was there again.

"It's going to be okay, baby. I'll jump on the jet and will be there the moment you two clear customs." Now it was my turn to choke back emotion. "I can't wait to have you in my arms again. See if you can get some sleep. Turn off your phone. We'll have the concierge at the Savoy handle the communication about flights. If we need to talk, I'll have someone knock on your door."

"David?" Ellen's voice was soft, small, afraid. "Did I hurt you?"

She had. But that didn't matter anymore.

"No matter what you do, I will still love you. Go to bed, my love. Take a Xanax if you have to. It will all be over soon."

"Thank you, David. Thank you for loving me."

"In less than twenty-four hours, I'll be doing precisely that. Now go to bed!"

"David?"

"Yes, sweetheart."

"Can you do me a favor?"

"Anything."

"I know why Adrian came over tonight. Take care of one another for me."

"We'll have a lot to talk about, for sure."

"You know exactly what I mean, David. Do I have to be specific? Do the nasty dance. Fuck her until she begs for mercy. It will be good for both of you."

"On one condition, my sweet."

"What's that?"

"Save the last dance for me."

For the first time that night, Ellen giggled.

On that note, she rang off.

Adrian was finishing up with the travel agent.

We stared at each other, cell phones in hands, totally nude. The tableau was so incredible that we both laughed. I felt the tension release. I now knew exactly what to do.

Adrian shrugged. "So much for the fuck-a-thon. I guess you better get some sleep, too, big boy. By this time tomorrow, you'll be riding a wildcat. I suddenly feel like yesterday's fish."

I dropped my phone onto the nightstand and put my hands behind Adrian's neck, pulling her toward me, planting a long, passionate kiss on her delicious mouth.

"You are the best friend two people could ever hope for, Adrian. I think a multi-course seafood meal is appropriate before you go."

Adrian's eyes widened as she saw what was rising in my lap.

"I just heard the reconciliation of the century, and you are doing this?"

"It was Ellen's idea. In fact, if she were here, it would probably be another memorable threesome."

Adrian's pulled me on top of her.

"I am suddenly incredibly wet and so horny for you that if you don't fuck me right this moment, David Orion, I might just die in your arms."

I looked down toward her legs. The mattress told the story of her soaked interest.

"Where's the velcro?"

"Put on a raincoat and make me feel beautiful," Adrian said.

I reached for the replica of the teakwood condom case I knew she remembered from our first meeting.

"Pick a winner," I said. "Let's see how many times I can make you come before sunrise."

27

LEGACY

One Year Later

DAVID

The limo driver was at the baggage claim in Denver to meet me.

"Ms. Corbin regrets that she couldn't come to the airport to greet you in person, sir. She will meet you at the restaurant at six o'clock as planned. Would you like to stop by your hotel beforehand?"

The driver waited outside The Brown Place Hotel as I showered and changed into my dinner attire. I assumed we would end up at Ellen's house, but she always gave me my space, just in case I wanted it.

I nodded. The limo pulled away from the arrivals concourse and onto the long asphalt ribbon that connected the airport to civilization.

"And by the way, sir," the driver said. "Happy Anniversary."

IN THE TWELVE MONTHS THAT HAD FOLLOWED ELLEN'S nightmare in London, all the dominos had started to fall in our favor. Fleet Street savaged Damon for blowing his chance with "England's Most Beloved American Royal." The publicity supercharged Corbin Cosmetics sales on both sides of the Atlantic. Her company stock split and was still one of the hottest buy recommendations on Wall Street.

A few weeks after Ellen had returned, I got a call from Robert Haden's secretary. He was requesting a personal meeting at his office at my convenience.

This meeting differed greatly from our first experience. The deal that Mandy had proposed turned out to be a winner. The Haden Corporation now stood on a firm foothold in the Asian market, creating thousands of new jobs and the cash flow that came with them.

Haden told me that one condition he insisted upon was that Mandy be named Haden Corporation's Vice President for Asian Operations, reporting directly to him. In his vast office, the hunting trophies were gone, replaced by mural-sized photographs of The Haden Institute for Aquatic Medicine. Monica Haden, DVM, had earned the degree she wanted. The world's finest aquatic vets would mentor her until she built up enough experience to take over as director. She and Frank now lived together near the Institute in the cottage she had bought with her own money.

"Nobody I have ever met has so profoundly changed my life," Robert Haden told me. "If there is ever anything I can do for you, just say the word."

I tried to convince him that his generosity had already surpassed my expectations, but he wasn't having it. When I held out a hand at the end of our visit, he wrapped his arms around me in an enormous bear hug. It felt as if my father had returned to life and was embracing me.

I gave Haden the chance to return that favor about eight months later when CeCe asked me to come to Arizona to discuss her next chapter. She wanted to open up a manufacturing plant in Thailand to create high-end accessories for women, made of recycled cans and plastics by former prostitutes, whom she hoped to recruit on the streets personally.

"It's an idea that's been done before, so I know it has legs," she told me. "But I know nothing about how to build and run a business. Do you know someone who might mentor me?"

I did.

Within the year, the first items in the "Thai Constellation Collection" were ready for market. Robert Haden himself had taken CeCe under his wing, funding the bulk of the enterprise and engaging his friends to direct some of their philanthropy in CeCe's direction.

The "Constellation" part, CeCe, confided in me, sounded better than "Orion."

"But," she said, kissing me on the cheek as she dropped me off at the airport, "you will always be my guiding star, David."

"And I'll always honor you, CeCe. Thank you for helping me find the courage to be vulnerable."

She gave me one last inspection. The memory of our evening together seemed to ripple through her. "Damn, I'll never forget that night."

After our final romp, Adrian left Sandia Wealth Advisers to work for Ellen full time as Corbin Cosmetic's Chief Operating Officer.

Amy became the sister I always wanted. She courted her soul-mate just as we had courted one another—slowly, confidently, and trusting the universe. The universe delivered, and he was eventually smitten. It was still too early to tell if it would last.

My favorite foster father had found his soul mate. I was best man, and Ellen was maid of honor when Elliot and Kimberly tied the knot, surrounded by five beaming foster kids.

Laura turned out to be the last of my clients. My next appointment at the bar never showed. After experiencing one hundred and forty-seven different women, I knew exactly what I wanted. I followed Adrian's advice, becoming a freelance stock analyst. When my former clients learned of my new career, every one of them became customers.

THE VESTA IS ONE OF DENVER'S MOST ROMANTIC RESTAURANTS. Named after the Roman Goddess of the Hearth, it was in perfect alignment with Ellen's brand. In the years since our first meeting, Ellen had grown from a frightened divorcee to the CEO of her own worldwide cosmetics firm. With Adrian's financial guidance, revenues crossed two billion dollars per year, and the company's stock price was soaring.

Among Ellen's most popular fragrances for men was the one she had named after me. "The alluring scent of sensuality" was the tag line I saw whenever the huge Corbin Cosmetics ad appeared on the screens in New York's Times Square. It accounted for fifteen percent of the company's gross revenues.

Such was her net worth that Ellen returned every dollar of her divorce settlement, with interest, to her ex-husband with a note that said, "Thanks for the seed money. I hope you are happy with your return on the investment."

At Vesta, they ushered me to a quiet table, an ice-cold Coca-Cola awaiting me. At six sharp, Ellen arrived.

She was now one of the world's most recognized personalities, pursued by the rich and famous, her products endorsed by Hollywood's most influential celebrities. All eyes were on her as she walked toward me.

I was so proud of the woman she was becoming.

As Ellen and I embraced, I felt our mystical connection. Fame and fortune had not changed her. It was still just the two of us, totally focused on one another, wordless communication flowing between.

As she sat, I produced a small box and set it in front of her. Her heart-melting smile appeared, and she produced a similar box from her purse.

"Always on the same wavelength," she said. "I'm so glad you came."

"The day we met changed my life, Ellen. And look at you! You're not that lost soul with a cable TV problem anymore."

"Open it," she said, pointing to the box in front of me.

"You know me," I responded. "Ladies first."

What she saw when she unwrapped my gift was a simple gold chain with a heart-shaped pendant. I had inscribed two Es on it. When she opened it, there was an engraving of both Ellen and Elise from the year we first met. Where the pendant would touch her chest were the words, "I will still love you."

A magnitude of memories flooded over us. Time stood still. We held hands across the table and stared into one another's eyes.

It was Ellen, the executive who brought me back to earth.

"Open yours, David. There's a question that comes with it."

Inside my box was an eighteen-carat gold band, a wedding band, embedded with Xs and Os around the outside. Our shared connection was what she had written on the inside.

"I will still love you."

Ellen was always the intuitive one in our relationship, able to discern my every thought.

"No, my love. This isn't another marriage proposal."

I felt a murmur of disappointment. "I know that your adventures in England didn't turn out the way you hoped. Do you ever wish we were married?"

Ellen grasped my hand. "Once you have a true soulmate, your heart is closed to everyone else. I know we've always talked about the age difference, and that night at the engagement party, I realized that marrying anybody but you would ruin this perfect union we truly share. And how about you? You never told me what happened with Amy."

"She wasn't you. That first day I saw you on Spring Street, I knew in my heart that I found my one true love."

There was more that I wanted to tell her. "You know that I traded my unique profession for something more utilitarian. And I'll share something. I don't miss it."

"Why is that, my love?"

"Every relationship you have encouraged me to explore has re-affirmed one thing. I don't want to please anyone else but you. I like the space we give one another; I would never demand your time or attention. Elise should always come first in that department. But I cherish every moment I spend with you. As we've grown together, that's the one clear thing—I'm yours. Supporting you and Elise is my life's purpose. Pleasing you is my life's work. It just took me time to figure it out."

I remembered her mysterious remark when she put the box in front of me. "So, if it isn't marriage, what is the question?"

It felt like Ellen had suddenly lost her nerve. She signaled for the waiter. "We'll talk about it later."

⚜

HER SENSE OF STYLE ONLY SURPASSED ELLEN'S BUSINESS ACUMEN. The dream house in the mountains mirrored Frank Lloyd Wright's "Falling Water" design, augmented and updated to meet her requirements. It wasn't as big as the house she still owned back home. A Colorado address was another dream come true. And Ellen was in the business of making dreams a reality.

After I wore Elise out with our usual combination of board games and basketball, I carried her into her bedroom to tuck her in.

"I love you, Uncle D," she said as she yawned. "I wish you lived with us all the time."

Over the years, Elise had become my de facto daughter. I attended every important event and spent some long nights in conversation with Ellen as she had dealt with the inevitable roller coaster ride that is parenting. Elise's biological father had re-married, and his new family didn't seem to want to include his miracle girl. I felt bad for what he was missing as this precious little lady navigated the wonder years. But I was also grateful to share them with her mother, my life partner, in every sense.

I pulled the covers around her shoulders and kissed her forehead.

"I love you, chipmunk. Wherever I may be, know that my heart is always with you and your mom."

Elise closed her eyes. A wicked smirk crossed her face. "You said that to me in London, Uncle D. Are we playing movie star again?"

I stroked a finger along the bridge of her nose.

"Sweet dreams, my little movie star. You will always be my favorite leading lady."

I noticed Ellen's shadow in the doorway. Her face was a portrait of contentment. But there was something else I saw. It was something new.

Ellen's bedroom boasted a breathtaking view of the Rocky Mountains. On the ceiling above the bed, tiny LED spotlights recreated the constellation that bore my last name. Ellen always said she enjoyed drifting off to sleep with me on top of her. Walls that weren't covered with windows had a log-cabin finish that gave the place a rustic feel.

But none of that was in my field of view as we lay across from one another. My love was now in her forties, but she looked ten years younger. Every detail of the exquisite body I knew so well was still firm and fit. A few battle scars from her executive life told stories in the tiny wrinkles that creased her forehead. But anyone who didn't know Ellen well would conclude that she was the same age as the day we had met.

"Now that we no longer have any distractions, what did you want to ask me?"

"Have you thought about the legacy you want to leave, David?"

It was an odd question. I was still working with Adrian to build that legacy. I was healthy, full of ideas and energy. What might endure after my earthly adventures were over never crossed my mind.

"I hope to have touched enough lives positively to have made a difference."

Ellen's alluring laugh bubbled up again. "Oh, you've already done that."

"What are you asking, my love? How can I please you?"

As Ellen inhaled, I imagined her remembering the first time I had said those words.

"You still arouse me, my love. I guess there's no other way to say this than to be direct. I want Elise to have a sibling. If I'm going to bring another child into the world, it needs to be soon. And there's only one person I want to help me create a new life."

Her delicate fingers touched my cheek.

"David, would you consider being the father of our child?"

Of all the questions Ellen might have asked, that one was the furthest from my mind. Ellen stood on the mountaintop of success. Her days were overflowing with activity. I had trouble imagining how she might make the enormous commitment to a new life at this point in her career

I didn't know what to say.

Her eyes were glistening. I felt as if my head was spinning.

"I can't imagine a world without you, David. All the good things that have happened to me have their roots in us. It's taken me way too long to realize it, but you are the one true love of my life. You are my greatest gift. I want to pass that gift on in the most wonderful way I know how."

I held that dazzling face in my hands, intoxicated by the emotion that flowed from her eyes.

"Are you sure, Ellen? Are you absolutely sure?"

"The two of us as one, David. Can you imagine anything more beautiful? I've never been surer of anything. I have a great leadership team and am ready to get back some of that life balance we argued about all those years ago. I want to be the mother of our child. But this has to be your call. We've always lived as interdependent equals and have made our own decisions. This is one that has to be unanimous."

I reached over her to the place on her nightstand where she always kept a condom for me. I picked up the silver square and held it before her in my open palm.

"Our love is my most precious treasure. You've encouraged a profession that has exposed me to many women. Each has more deeply affirmed that you are the one woman I have truly loved and the only person with whom I want to share life's journey. What's the saying? 'Getting married is just an affirmation of something that already exists.' We've really been partners since the day we met. I wouldn't want it any other way. "

I took aim and tossed the condom toward the wastebasket, making a perfect shot from three-point territory.

"Since that first day, I've wanted to do this without one of those damn things," I said. "Let's find out what it feels like."

Ellen's eyes instantly filled with tears. "Thank you, my love. Once again, you say just the right thing at just the right moment. I promise to prioritize our two children. Yes, Elise is as much your daughter as she is mine. And I'm ready to make this a night we will both remember forever."

Being inside of Ellen without the barrier of birth control was indescribable. There was no foreplay and very little friction. We simply embraced, gazing into one another's eyes, two hearts beating as one. Her powerful muscles massaged me. She was glowing. Her aura radiated joy, satisfaction, peace.

It didn't take long. I thought about the many experiences we shared and how, despite our mutual independence, we were truly a partnership in every important way.

She called out a command to the Amazon Echo device on her nightstand.

I could hear John Denver's familiar twelve-string guitar as "The Eagle and the Hawk" played over the bedroom audio system.

When the last two lyrics came around, she sang the first one softly. "Reach for the heavens and hope for the future."

I knew them, too, and finished the verse, kissing her neck as I whispered them into her ear.

"And all that we can be and not what we are."

The orchestra behind John Denver's guitar began its final crescendo.

It was time.

"Are you ready, Ellen?" I asked.

"I'm ready."

Without taking my eyes off of her, I let go, filling Ellen with the true essence of new life. She pulled my gift upward toward her own contribution that was waiting to receive it.

We lay together as one to be sure that nature would take its course. But in that one moment of release, we both knew that, for better or worse, for richer, for poorer, in sickness and in health, our once-in-a-lifetime love would endure, as long as we both might live.

28

THE SOUNDTRACK

David's Theme

"Roll to Me" – Del Amitri 1995 A&M Records

Laura

"Sledgehammer" – Peter Gabriel 1986 Warner Music Group

Ellen

"I Feel the Earth Move" – Mandy Moore 2003 Epic Records

"Everything That Touches You" – The Association 1967 Warner Records Inc.

Dating

"Owner of a Lonely Heart" – Yes 1983 Atlantic Recording Corp

A Return Engagement

"Day After Day" – Rod Stewart 2006 SME

Moondance

"Moondance" – Nathan East w/ Michael MacDonald 2104 Warner Music Group

Adrian

"Beautiful" – Gordon Lightfoot 1994 Reprise Records

Pillow Talk

"Haven't Got Time for the Pain" – Carly Simon – 1942 Warner Music Group

Monica

"Shake It Off" – Tim Akers & The Smoking Section 2014 Big Machine Records

"I'll Lead You Home" – Michael W. Smith 1995 Reunion Records

What is Happening to Me?

"I Can't Explain" – Yvonne Elliman 2016 Purple Records

Meeting Mr. Haden

"Roll With the Changes" – REO Speedwagon 1978 Epic Records

Ellen Struggles with My Age

"Every Day Is a Winding Road" – Sheryl Crow 1996 A&M Records

Kimberly

"Feeling Stronger Every Day" – Leonid & Friends 1973 Rhino Entertainment Company

Kimberly – Part 2

"Swayin' To The Music" – Johnny Rivers 1977 Exploration Group

Saturday

"Something About You" – Level 42 – 1985 Polydor Records

Swimming with the Dolphins

"East of Ginger Trees" – Seals and Crofts 1972 Rhino Entertainment Company

Mandy

"Let It Grow" – Eric Clapton 1974 Universal International Music B.V.

Our First Fight

"Room to Move" – Animotion 1984 Polydor Records

"I Will Still Love You" – Stonebolt 1978 Casablanca Music Group

Damon and Eva

"Kind of a Drag" (Acapella) – Buckinghams 1967 Columbia Records

"Lady" – Little River Band 1978 Warner Music Group

Trusting the Universe

"Don't You Worry Bout a Thing" – Jacob Collier 2013 Jacob Collier

Amy

"For the First Time" – Kenny Loggins 1996 Columbia Records

The Last Dance?
"Sunshine" - John Denver - RCA Records 1973
Meeting Damon's Ex
"What Becomes of the Broken Hearted" - Jimmy Ruffin 1965 Motown Records

"Fool if You Think It's Over" – Chris Rea 1988 Entertainment Company
Adrian - Part 2
"Second Avenue" – Tim Moore 1974 Warner Music Group
Legacy
"Express Yourself" – Madonna 1989 Sire Records

"The Eagle and the Hawk" – John Denver 1973 BMG
Ending Credits
"Save the Last Dance for Me" – Michael Bublé' Warner Music Group

ACKNOWLEDGMENTS

Editors can turn passable prose into compelling tales. Stacy Donovan and Stephie Walls improved this story immensely. I'm grateful for their gifts.

This baby had more beta readers than I have space to thank. Each contributed gems which added to the authenticity of Ellen, David and the cast. Thank you all.

Please Her began as a single chapter, written on a bet. I won the bet and 27 chapters later, it was a book.

It should go without saying, but this is a work of fiction. Names, characters, places, and incidents either are products of my imagination or are used fictitiously. Any resemblance to actual events or persons, living or dead, is entirely coincidental.

Thanks for coming along for the ride!
MacKenzie Masters
Seattle, Washington - 2021